THE NORTH KOREA ONYX

An Ainsley Walker Gemstone Travel Mystery

J.A. JERNAY

PLOTWORKS PUBLISHING

WARNING

This story contains a scene of graphic violence in Chapter 39. Audience discretion is advised.

Our enemies are the American bastards
Who are trying to take over our beautiful fatherland
With guns that I make with my own hands
I will shoot them.
BANG, BANG, BANG!

—"Shoot the Yankee Bastards," a popular North Korean children's song

CHAPTER ONE

Ainsley Walker stepped out of the taxicab and looked at the note in her hand. It read Korean Christian Church of Worshippers.

Then she looked at the structure before her.

It was an old gray bungalow, its wide porch sagging on the either end like a frown. Rusted vertical bars jammed down into the windowsills like sad hands into pockets. A black barred fence circled the property, and a hammered metal sign featured a series of letters that she couldn't understand.

She matched the addresses. This was the place.

It was a surprise. Catholics built elaborate peaked structures with rich iconography, Protestants built large warehouses with plain walls, Mormons prided themselves on pristine white temples. But this church was basically four walls and a roof. That didn't mean these people were less religious. It just meant they were poor.

A small button was affixed to the post on the side of the gate. Ainsley pushed it and waited for the sound of a bell. Nothing. It was broken.

She cupped her hands around her mouth. "Hello?"

In a window, a curtain flipped aside. The outline of a figure appeared, a spurt of foreign language burbled out. Then the front door jerked open, and an Asian man stepped onto the porch. He was of medium height and average build.

"Who is it?"

"I'm looking for the Korean Christian Church of Worshippers," Ainsley replied.

"What is your name?"

There wasn't any warmth in his voice. No trust either. But he hadn't said it was the wrong place.

"Ainsley Walker."

"Who?"

She raised her voice, almost to a shout. "My name is Ainsley Walker. You contacted me about a job. We have an appointment."

The man turned and leaned over to speak to somebody. She'd worked with enough tentative clients in the past to recognize the moment when the tribe would decide whether or not to crack open the gate. This was that moment.

Finally, the man came out onto the porch and down the steps. He was slightly stooped, with a short nest of black hair cropped firmly around his skull. His face was ordinary but inscrutable.

"Thank you for coming," he said. His softly accented syllables splatted onto the ground like spoonfuls of pudding.

"My pleasure," she replied.

He unlatched the gate from the inside. She could've reached through the slats and done the same but had decided to show respect.

"My name is Pastor Jeong," he said.

They shook hands, and he dipped his head a little. Ainsley did the same. She never knew the exact protocol for meeting Asian people—except that it varied by nationality—so she usually just copied whatever they did.

She followed him through the front yard. It was clean, the hedges trimmed, the footpath paved nicely. There was a meticulous mind here. That was good. It meant that whoever owned the mind had thought this assignment through.

Ainsley was starting to feel intrigued.

Stepping onto the porch, she felt the floorboards sag beneath her feet.

"Please enter," said Pastor Jeong. He was holding open the front door with an outstretched arm.

Taking a breath, Ainsley stepped inside. The walls were simple eggshell-white plaster. A portrait of a Caucasian-looking Jesus hung opposite the front door. To her left, in what used to be a living room, sat four rows of folding chairs before a small podium. The pungent smell of a cleaning solution reached her nose.

The interior matched the exterior. Orderly. Ainsley liked that too. No false fronts.

She became aware of the faces watching her. There were seven—large adult faces regarding her coolly, small children's faces peering at her halfway around corners. They all featured the same moonish shape, the same high cheekbone ridges.

"Please," said Pastor Jeong.

His hand was pointing at Ainsley's feet. Then she noticed the shoes stacked triple-deep alongside the door. She'd forgotten about this custom.

Ainsley lifted her left leg, balancing on her right like a stork, and used her right thumb and forefinger to tug down the zipper of her calf-high brown leather boot. It wouldn't budge.

"I have to sit down," she said.

"Of course," said Pastor Jeong.

Ainsley lowered herself to the floor. Her jeans were jammed tightly inside of her boots. As her fingers fumbled with the zipper, she was aware of the faces watching her.

She would've given anything for a bench. This was undignified.

At last she tugged the boots off, and the pastor barked something. A child scampered forward and laid two foam slippers at her feet.

"Thank you," said Ainsley.

She slid her feet into the foam slippers, and awkwardly pulled herself up from the floor.

"We will talk in the prayer room," said Pastor Jeong.

"That's fine with me."

They entered the space. A tambourine and a guitar stood against one wall. Several black hymnals with Korean characters written in gold leaf on the side were stacked neatly in one corner. A poster of an outstretched hand beneath a rainbow reminded the congregation that God was watching over all of his children.

The man gestured to the chair next to the podium. "Please, sit there."

Ainsley approached the dais and lowered herself into the seat. The seven others filed into the room and sat down in the folding chairs. Nobody sat in the front row, not even Pastor Jeong.

All of them faced her silently. Ainsley felt her palms moisten. This was shaping up to be more a spiritual interrogation than a job interview.

"Before we discuss the assignment," Pastor Jeong said, "I have to ask you a question."

"Okay."

His eyes met her own. "Do you like to run?"

CHAPTER TWO

Ainsley stared at the minister. He had folded his arms and leaned back in his chair. His feet were crossed at the ankles.

"That's a strange question," she said. "Do I like to run?"

"Yes."

"It depends on what type of running are you talking about. From the police?"

She waited for laughter, but the joke fell on deaf ears.

"I mean competitive running," he said.

There was no way that this pastor could've known, but Ainsley had enjoyed a long history of success in track-and-field. None of it was applicable to her current career as an international gemstone detective, which is why she'd always left it off her résumé.

"As a matter of fact," she replied, "you've called the right person."

"How so?"

"I've been a runner all my life. I was all-state in track-and-field for all four years of high school. Mostly sprints, though."

His eyes grew slightly wider. A tiny smile cracked his inscrutable face. "Really?"

"Yes."

The Korean minister uncrossed his feet. His eyes roamed the wall behind her head. "And do you continue to enjoy running?"

"Yes, three times a week."

The Korean minister lifted a finger to his lips, deep in thought. She wasn't sure how her answers had caused such an intense state of reflection. It was probably just his nature. He was the type of man who could ponder the eternal mystery of a paperclip.

"This church is not very wealthy," he said.

"How many members do you have?"

"Thirty-one. It used to be thirty-six but we lost a family last year."

Ainsley nodded. That sort of loss could sink a precarious organization like this one. It was no different from a startup, except that instead of being lured by extravagant stock options, its immigrant members were lured by the hope of survival.

She looked around the room. "How long have you been here?"

"We arrived four years ago. With God's help we will continue to prosper."

The other people stirred in their seats. She doubted their English skills, but Ainsley sensed that they understood the phrase with God's help.

"People need each other when times are tough," she said. "Now, can you tell me about the assignment?"

"This job is potentially dangerous," he replied, "and it requires some training."

In her head, alarm bells went off. Ainsley knew instinctively that this man wasn't an exaggerator. If he said it was dangerous, he meant it.

"What is it?"

He delivered the answer gently. "You will be running a marathon."

"Why?"

"Because it's the only way you can enter the country."

Inside her chest, Ainsley felt that small creature known as curiosity perk up its ears, stretch its arms, and rise to its feet. "Which country are you talking about, Pastor Jeong?"

The minister delivered the answer as though it were the most natural place to visit in the world.

"North Korea," he said.

CHAPTER THREE

Ainsley felt the blood begin to drain out of her head. Her hands clenched the handles on the side of her chair. Her mouth worked itself open and shut, trying to find words.

There weren't any. This was unprecedented. She'd been sent to some strange foreign countries in the past—but never to a place like that.

North Korea. The Hermit Kingdom. The most oppressive society on earth.

All for a marathon.

Ainsley had found herself traveling on some pretty weird pretexts before. But running a marathon was entirely new ground. And she didn't yet understand how any of this related to a gemstone.

"I need to repeat this," she said. "You want me to run a marathon in North Korea?"

The minister nodded. He turned his head and spoke to the people seated behind him. An elderly woman stood up and shuffled down the aisle, her head bowed low, and handed Ainsley a folded piece of newspaper. It was an article from an English-language newspaper.

The headline: Pyongyang Opens Annual Marathon to International Competitors.

"This is for real?" she said.

"Yes."

"It's hard to believe."

"You can believe it," said the minister.

Ainsley folded the paper and put it into her bag. "What does this have to do with me? I'm a gemstone investigator."

"You will be recovering a gemstone," he said.

"How?"

"I cannot tell you that."

She tried a different angle. "What type of gemstone is it?"

"I cannot tell you that either."

"But why a marathon?"

He grew a touch impatient. "As I already explained, it's the only way we can to get you into the country."

"There has to be a reason to enter North Korea?"

A shadow darkened the minister's face. "I see that you are not familiar with that country."

"I know that it's a really bad place."

He nodded. "Yes, and the regime strictly controls all visitors."

"You mean I would have to check in with somebody every couple of days?"

He cleared his throat and edged forward on his seat. Ainsley could see that he was getting impatient with her.

"Miss Walker, you will be under constant scrutiny."

"By cameras?"

The minister grew more emphatic. "No, by people. You will have government minders every hour of the day, and they will move you around. They will tell you where to go, what to do. All the freedom that you enjoy here in the West will be gone."

"Okay," she said, "I understand."

He stood up and handed Ainsley an envelope. She reached over the first row of folding chairs and accepted it. Her name had been written on the front.

"That is your contract," said the minister.

Ainsley felt the weight of it in her hand. "I have another question."

"Yes."

"Why don't you send someone who speaks the language? Someone who blends in better than I do?"

The pastor visibly willed himself to stay patient. "Because we are citizens of South Korea."

"So?"

"Please understand," he said, "citizens of South Korea are prohibited from entering North Korea. There is no official relationship between the two countries."

His hands illustrated the gap. Ainsley didn't know what to say. Part of her wondered if she should suggest that they hire another Asian—maybe a Chinese, or a Malay—someone who could blend in. Then she thought better. Population groups were always the best judges of who belonged and who didn't. A Vietnamese person would look just as out of place in North Korea as a Caucasian person would.

"I would like you to read the contract," the minister said, "and let me know what you think."

"When do you need an answer?"

"By tomorrow night."

Ainsley stood up and slung her bag over her shoulder. "Then I will call you tomorrow night."

The minister stood too. "Thank you for coming to visit us."

He escorted Ainsley out of the room, past the few people in the chairs. They watched her go.

At the front door, she pulled on her boots and then stood

up again. As she shook Pastor Jeong's hand, he held her grip for a moment. He studied her palm.

"What is it?"

"You have large hands," he said, "for a woman."

"I do?"

He nodded. "It will be useful on this assignment." A mysterious smile lit up his face. "Have a good night, Miss Walker."

He opened the front door, and as Ainsley walked down the path to the gate, she wondered what he meant by that.

CHAPTER FOUR

Six o'clock in the morning, and Ainsley was already on her sixteenth and final lap on the track.

It was the end of her six point four kilometer run. She'd been aiming for twenty-eight minutes. She glanced at her wristwatch. It read 27:05. That meant that she had fifty-five seconds to finish the final lap. That was a tall order for anybody, let alone a twenty-nine-year-old woman who'd just run fifteen previous laps, but she was determined.

Ainsley Walker didn't like to fail.

A month ago, she'd changed her exercise pattern. Instead of sweating in a hot yoga room, or wiping down nautilus equipment, she'd begun long distance running. It'd been a first for her, since she'd been a sprinter all her life. She'd embarked on this with an eye on finishing a half-marathon in two months' time. She'd even purchased new super light-weight running shoes, new shorts, new everything.

It was a lucky choice, given the weird assignment that had just landed in her lap.

As she turned the final curve and the final lap, she increased her speed. Sweat from her upper lip seeped into her mouth and leaked salty on her tongue. Her arms and legs moved in fluid rhyme. It felt good to accelerate.

Glancing over, she saw David Madradis on the bleachers, eyeglasses on his face, studying her paperwork. He was her occasional exercise partner and legal sounding board. He'd only run three point two kilometers, because he'd promised to spend a few minutes looking over the contract that she needed help with.

Ainsley had always taken his help as a sign of his sympathy for the way that her husband, the Legal Weasel, had backed out of the marriage. The two of them had been classmates during law school, and both David and Ainsley had felt betrayed by the way that he'd fled their lives with no notice.

At last Ainsley lunged across the finish line, pushing her torso forward, the way that shaves a couple of milliseconds in a tournament when there is video coverage of the finish line.

As she slowed down to a walk, Ainsley looked down at her stopwatch. It read 28:12. She'd missed her goal by twelve seconds.

She drew in a huge breath of air, her cheeks blown out like a puffer fish, and then exhaled through her lips. She lifted her arms over her head, tipped her face to the sky to improve oxygen intake, and walked halfway around the track. Then she headed back to the bleachers.

She collapsed on the bleacher next to David. He scooted himself several feet down.

"I know I'm gross," she said.

"It's just that my wife has a nose like a bloodhound," he replied. "I mean, she can tell when my assistant changes the coffee from hazelnut to dark roast."

Ainsley laughed. "But your wife likes me."

"She does, but she's got a hell of a powerful jealousy gene. Woe be to the man who triggers it. Give me thirty seconds."

Ainsley picked up a squeeze bottle and sent a stream of

water shooting down her throat. Then she toweled off her face.

When David had finished, he scowled and slapped the document with the back of his hand. "This has to be the most poorly written legal document I've seen."

"They're Korean immigrants, David."

"That doesn't mean they have to be unprofessional. I mean, listen to this." He read from the document. "'The origination of the operative will keep secret the faster time of the purpose.'" He looked up. "It sounds like spam."

Ainsley laughed. "Oh, cut them some slack."

"No. It sounds like my four-year-old daughter wrote it with crayon on a wall."

Ainsley felt her heart rate slowing now, her core temperature beginning to cool. "Tell me something good about the contract," she said.

David Madradis weighed the document in his hand. "I don't speak moron, but from what I can tell, it looks like they're going to pay you nicely. And they're going to provide airfare, hotel, as well as the cost of entering the marathon. It's an interesting assignment."

"Definitely."

"And I've heard that Seoul is really hip."

Ainsley looked at him curiously. "Seoul is in South Korea."

"Isn't that where they're sending you?" He consulted the paper. "This, how do you say it? Mangyongdae Marathon?"

"It's in Pyongyang."

His eyes searched hers for a moment. "You're going to Pyongyang?"

"Yes."

"The capital of North Korea?"

"Yes."

"You're kidding me."

She shook her head no.

He took off his glasses and pinched the bridge of his nose and then stared at something invisible on the horizon. "They want to send you to North Korea to run a marathon."

"It's not as crazy as it seems."

"But where's the gemstone?" He poked the document with his finger. "It's not even mentioned."

Ainsley shrugged. "The pastor won't tell me anything more until I agree to the deal."

The lawyer ran a hand through his hair. "Last year I went to a conference. It was one of those institutes-for-continuing-legal-education types of things."

"And?"

"I took an international law seminar, just for fun. One of the speakers talked about North Korea for almost twenty-five minutes. I won't go into any detail, but let's just say it's not a place you want to go. For any reason."

"I know that."

His eyes held her own. "If you get in trouble there, you are beyond totally screwed. Remember those two journalists?"

Ainsley did remember. A few years earlier, a pair of American television reporters had been caught illegally trespassing in North Korea, and it had taken nothing less than a former president of the United States, flying to Pyongyang on a private jet, to secure their release. Other Westerners hadn't been so fortunate.

"Yes," said Ainsley, "but they were trespassing. I'm just running a marathon."

"You don't know that," said David. "It doesn't matter anyways. All the rules of Western civil society don't exist there. If they want to imprison you, they'll imprison you. You're nothing more than a pawn that the regime can use in its game of international blackmail."

Ainsley looked glumly at the empty track, her shoulders

slumped. "If you're trying to scare me, you're doing a good job."

"Let me describe it a different way," he said. "You ever read 1984? By George Orwell?"

"Yes."

"You remember any of it?"

Ainsley scrunched up her nose, thinking back to high school. "Not really."

"Big Brother, endless war, total propaganda? Winston and Julia? The last sentence—He loved Big Brother. Nothing rings a bell?"

"Yeah, a little."

His hand found her shoulder. "That's North Korea, Ainsley. We looked at that book as a nightmare. They looked at that book as a blueprint."

Ainsley nodded. Deep down, she knew how totally foolish it would be to accept this assignment.

"Now, about this contract," he said. "Are you really planning to sign it?"

"I am."

"Then at least allow me to represent you. Somebody needs to hammer this out with the Korean Christian Church of Worshippers."

"David, I can't afford to pay you."

He smiled. "What are the two most beautiful words in the English language?"

"I don't know."

"Pro bono." He clapped her on the knee, then stood up. "I'll talk to my colleague Daniel Cho. He's young, bilingual, smart as a whip. He'll do whatever I ask."

Ainsley felt herself melting a little inside. It was good to know that somebody had her back when she needed it.

She stood up and moved towards him, arms out. "You're getting a hug, whether you like it or not."

David quickly backed away, holding palms up. "No, you're still disgusting."

She laughed in spite of herself. "Just because you're helping me doesn't give you the right to be an ass."

"Sure it does. I'll call you tonight."

He turned and ran down the steps of the bleachers towards his car, her contract tucked underneath his arm. Ainsley watched him go, smiling.

CHAPTER FIVE

As the little boy leaped off the swing and fell face-first into the rubber playground mat, Ainsley was afraid that she'd killed him.

She clapped her hands to her cheeks. "Oh my God, I didn't mean to do that, he just, oh no, I am so sorry!"

On a nearby bench, her friend Deirdre glanced over, barely concerned. Ainsley and Deirdre had been close for years, from their single party era all the way through marriage and now Deirdre's motherhood.

"Maybe you didn't get the news," said Deirdre, taking a drag on a cigarette, "but my kid is indestructible. Look."

Sure enough, the boy had pulled himself to his feet, a lunatic smile on his face.

"It'll be him and the cockroaches," said Ainsley.

"Wipe your face, sweetie," said Deirdre.

The boy climbed back into the swing. "Moooore!"

Ainsley began pushing him again. "He's never broken anything?"

"Not yet," her friend replied, immersed in her phone.

"Matt thinks he's going to be a stuntman, but I say a base jumper. He mostly likes to fall."

"Mothers know best."

Deirdre put the phone away. Her lips worked the cigarette while her eyes roved up and down Ainsley's figure. "So you've lost some weight."

"Nah."

"For sure in your shoulders. I can see your clavicles."

Ainsley's fingers touched her upper chest. Sure enough, she felt the delicate nubbin of bone just below her skin.

"I've been running a lot," she said.

"I bet you haven't been eating enough."

Ainsley grew a little defensive. "Of course I've been eating."

"Tell me everything you ate yesterday."

Only Deirdre was bold enough to confront her so openly. Ainsley tried to remember. She'd had a cup of yogurt for breakfast, an apple with string cheese for lunch, and chicken breast with steamed cauliflower for dinner. She'd also drunk two cups of coffee and eight cups of water.

"You know," she said, "it probably wasn't enough."

Deirdre smiled. "Remember that purple skirt you liked to wear when we used to go to Mandolina's? You had the cutest shape back then."

Ainsley resented the past tense, but she admitted that it was true. She'd lost a fair amount of weight since her husband had left her. Some people dealt with emotional stress by overindulging, gobbling slices of pizza, plates of nachos, slabs of cheesecake. Other people denied themselves, shutting down, drinking nothing but tea, turning inwards, becoming spiritual. Ainsley had been surprised to find that she was one of the latter.

"Deirdre," she said, "I don't look bad, do I?"

Her friends looked at her, squinting. "Parts of you look smaller."

Ainsley looked down. It was true. Her chest had shrunk, and there hadn't been much to lose anyways.

"Do you want me to tell Matt that you've been smoking?"

Deirdre immediately ground out the stub of the cigarette into the bench. "I'll deny everything." She glanced at her friend. "Look at it like this, Ainsley. Not all of us can lose fifteen pounds on our own."

A weird silence settled between them. Ainsley felt the jealousy hanging in the air like the smell of burning tires. On the other side of the swing set, Justin fell to the ground with another thud.

Ainsley wiped dirt from the boy's face and set him on his feet. "Deirdre, don't be like that. Your life is so much richer than mine. You have a beautiful son, a faithful husband, a nice house. A father that's still alive. I don't have any of those things."

Her friend grew a little indignant. "But you have adventure, Ainsley."

"So?"

"I want to choose adventure too."

Ainsley was at a loss for words. "Well, we can't have everything."

"Yes, I can."

"No," said Ainsley, "having it all was a lie that society told our mothers to make them neurotic. Besides, if you knew where I was going on my next assignment, you wouldn't be so jealous."

"Tell me."

"No."

"Then I'm going to guess," said Deirdre. "You're going to Italy."

"I said you wouldn't be jealous."

"Somewhere in the Middle East?"

"Try again."

"Africa?"

"You'll never guess."

The little boy took off like a shot across the playground. She and Deirdre followed, strolling across the grass. Ainsley looked at the new houses lining the park. Inside were clean showers with hot water, pantries laden with canned goods, nine hundred channels of cable on the widescreen.

She felt a swift pang of regret stab her. Maybe her friend had the right idea about life. Maybe it was better to be safe, stable, and comfortable.

"Tell me," said Deirdre.

Ainsley took a deep breath. "North Korea."

Her friend stopped walking. She looked as though Ainsley had just announced that she was having gender reassignment surgery.

"You're kidding me."

"No. And I'm going to run a marathon."

Her friend clutched her arm. "You can't go there. I mean, you don't know what things are like. It's not a normal place."

"Yeah, that's the point."

Growing more agitated, Deirdre clutched her elbow. "How are you going to eat, Ainsley? Those people are starving."

"It's a tour. They have to feed us."

"And a marathon? Oh my God, you're going to lose even more weight."

"I'll eat before I leave—"

Deirdre cut her off. "You're coming over for dinner tonight. I'm making a tuna fish casserole for Justin and you're going to eat whether you like it or—"

Ainsley's phone buzzed. She looked at the screen. It was a text message from David Madradis.

The new contract is ready. Pastor Jeong wants a meeting at the church tonight at seven o'clock.

"I can't tonight," said Ainsley.

"Why not?"

Ainsley put her phone back into her bag. "Because I've chosen adventure."

CHAPTER SIX

Ainsley arrived at the church promptly at seven o'clock pm. Standing at the front gate were David Madradis and a young Korean man she didn't recognize. He wore a gray suit with no tie and looked a little young for the outfit.

"Ainsley Walker," said David, "this is Daniel Cho. He graduated from University of Michigan law school three years ago. He's one of our top young associates."

"Thanks for helping," she said.

The young man shook her hand, then turned to the older attorney. "David, she doesn't look that crazy."

"Just get to know her better," the older attorney replied. Then he turned to Ainsley. "Daniel here spoke with Pastor Jeong."

Daniel cleared his throat. "He was very cooperative and together we made a better translation of the contract. In fact, we made two versions—one in English, one in Korean. Here you go." He handed her a manila folder. "And I got an extra two hundred dollars for you as well."

Ainsley was pleasantly surprised. "You are quite a negotiator."

"And so young," added David.

"I'm not that young," said Daniel.

David elbowed Ainsley. "The partners won't let him see the inside of a courtroom until his voice drops."

Ainsley could tell that the younger attorney was used to the ribbing. She opened the envelope and looked over the contract. The terms looked much better now. "So what can I do for you in return, Daniel?"

A shrewd look passed over his face. "You want to hear the answer?"

"Yes."

"Don't sign it."

Ainsley was startled. "You're serious?"

A heavy look settled on his face. "Going to North Korea is foolish. The relief workers don't even go there. They just go to China and wait to help the refugees who escape."

"But this isn't relief work," she said.

Daniel shrugged. "You can do what you want, but I think everybody should stay out of the country."

"And I think that I should reserve judgment until I know more about the assignment," she replied. "It'll make a great story someday."

"If you survive."

Ainsley ignored that and turned her attention towards the church. She could see Pastor Jeong watching them from inside the front door.

"We should go," said David, checking his watch. "My wife had dinner on the table twenty minutes ago."

Ainsley shook his hand. "I owe both of you."

"We'll collect someday," said David.

"The favor bank never forgets," added Daniel.

They shook her hand. She watched as they moved off down the street and got into their car and left.

Then Ainsley was alone in front of the small immigrant church.

Pastor Jeong came out of the house and down the front walk and opened the gate. "We are happy that you returned to us, Miss Walker."

"I want to learn more about this assignment," replied Ainsley.

"Let's go inside and I'll show you."

She followed him up the walk and into the house. The contract weighed heavy in her hand. This was starting to feel serious.

And dangerous.

After kicking off her shoes and accepting the foam slippers, Ainsley entered the main room. This time, it was full of Korean families—tired men, haggard women, noisy children. Ainsley did a quick head count. Thirty-one people. The church's entire congregation. All of them here for one reason.

Her.

Nearly every seat was occupied, except for one. The chair on the dais next to the podium.

She walked down the main aisle and seated herself before the congregation. Head high, back straight, feet crossed at the ankle, hands on lap.

Professional.

Pastor Jeong stood at the podium beside her, bowed his head, and began to murmur in a low voice. The congregants did the same. Ainsley realized that it was a prayer.

Then the minister said ah-men and looked up. "I introduce to you Miss Ainsley Walker. She is the gemstone investigator who will be helping us." He repeated it in Korean.

Ainsley felt alarmed. She hadn't taken the job—not yet.

Pastor Jeong continued: "The time is very dire for our community. We lost membership last year. Our utilities are past due. We cannot continue to exist for much longer."

Ainsley looked out at the faces. They appeared dismal, saddened—but not surprised. They knew the score.

"But there is still hope," he said. "God himself has sent Miss Walker, who will help our community to survive."

The faces turned towards Ainsley. She managed a weak smile. It wasn't every day that she was greeted as an emissary of divine intervention.

"Please bring in the machine," he said.

From the foyer came the sound of something heavy rattling. Into the room came a man pushing an old film projector on a long extension cord. He parked it halfway down the center aisle, then turned it to face the side wall.

"This footage is very old," said Pastor Jeong. "Lights off, please."

CHAPTER SEVEN

As the room was plunged into darkness, the man at the cart hoisted a movie reel onto the spokes of the projector. She watched him thread the ancient film around the spools.

"This film," said Pastor Jeong, "has been in my family for over sixty years."

Then the image suddenly appeared on the far wall. Everybody turned to watch. It looked to be an old black-and-white documentary—waves crashing against cold beaches, distant snow-capped peaks, rice paddies, clay pots in a field, broad peasant faces under enormous hats.

A narrator began to speak, but the film had degraded so much over sixty years that it was barely audible.

Then the film jumped to footage of an object.

A jet-black ceramic teacup.

A ring of Korean characters was printed in a band around its midsection. The item was sitting behind glass, in whose reflection Ainsley could see onlookers moving and jostling.

"Stop the film," said the minister.

The man stopped the machine, and the image of the dark teacup was pinned to the wall.

"This is a very rare artifact, Ainsley," said Pastor Jeong. "It's the only image of this teacup that exists in the West."

Ainsley studied the object. It looked like thousands of other teacups. She leaned forward and squinted her eyes. The poor quality of the film made it difficult to verify, but it seemed that the dark finish wasn't matte. It was glossy and reflective.

Then she saw something else. She peered closely. "Are those facets?"

The minister looked at her, his eyeglasses small disks of reflected white light. "What do you think, Miss Walker?"

"That's not ceramic."

The room fell silent except for the metal fan whirring inside the projector. Once again she became aware of the congregation's eyes upon her.

"No," replied the minister, "it's made of onyx. And we want you to find it."

CHAPTER EIGHT

Ainsley's eyebrows nearly lifted off her face as she studied the object again. It was as dark and as seductive as a handsome sociopath making eyes in the corner of a hotel lounge.

"That's an onyx?" she said.

"Yes."

Ainsley knew about that gemstone, and even owned a pair of onyx earrings. It was a banded form of chalcedony, usually formed into beads, cabochons, intaglios, and cameos. Contrary to popular opinion, most onyx isn't black. It only gained its dark reputation because, as an agate, it's easily darkened, an artificial process that humans have been performing for thousands of years. Even in the first century, Pliny the Elder had written about ways to artificially treat it. The first two books of the Bible, Genesis and Exodus, mention the stone too.

Ainsley turned back to the minister. "So you want me to find this? In North Korea?"

"Not exactly," he replied. "We already have it. We need you to retrieve it."

"How?"

"From this man."

Pastor Jeong handed Ainsley a small card. It was a copy of a passport photo. A heavy Korean face stared back at her. He had thick lips, wide nostrils, and a heavy gaze. Around his neck was a simple white-collar shirt with a necktie. It wasn't a dangerous or rebellious face. It was simply a determined face.

"His name is Kenneth Park. He's one of our church members. He went into North Korea three months ago to find it."

"And he was successful?"

"Yes."

"So why doesn't he bring it back himself?"

The minister grew somber. "He cannot leave. The regime found a Bible in his hotel room."

"Bibles aren't allowed?"

The minister shook his head.

"Now he cannot leave Pyongyang. He is living like a ghost, gliding from one building to another. We don't know exactly where he is."

Ainsley thought about the sacrifice this man had made. He was willing to plunge himself into one of the worst countries on earth, and potentially die in a North Korean prison, all to save his church.

Still, there was an unanswered question.

Why?

Other churches held bake sales and car washes. Why would this little immigrant church, on the brink of financial ruin, send one of its members into the worst country on earth to recover a simple onyx?

"This artifact must be valuable," she said.

"It's a Korean national treasure," Pastor Jeong replied. "It's worth almost two hundred thousand dollars."

"Do you already have a buyer?"

Pastor Jeong smiled. "Yes, we do."

Now things were coming into focus. "Can I ask who it is?"

"Ji-hoon Kwon."

The minister waited for that to sink in. It didn't. "Who is Ji-hoon Kwon?" she asked.

"The owner of the Kwon Group. He's one of the most famous Korean investors in the United States, worth over three hundred million dollars. He has a great personal interest in recovering this treasure."

"Why?"

"It would be a blow to the regime."

In Ainsley's mind, the clouds finally parted. She understood everything now. Pastor Jeong had constructed an elaborate scheme to extract a valuable treasure from the worst country on earth—all to save his church. And now that scheme had come to a standstill.

She raised her hand. "Another question. It's been hidden for sixty years, right?"

"Yes."

"Then why hasn't anybody else recovered it?"

"Two reasons. One, nobody knew where it was. Two, nobody was willing to buy it."

"So how did Kenneth Park know where it was?"

He sighed. "You are very thorough in your questioning."

"Wouldn't you be?"

The congregation remained silent as he began his explanation. "Before the war," Pastor Jeong said, "in the nineteen-forties, the onyx teacup used to belong to my family. My grandfather hid it just before Kim Il Sung came to power, and then he fled to the South. He always assumed that he would return to find it again. He didn't know how severe the division of the Korean people was going to be, or how long the division would last. Twenty-five years later he died, but he left my family detailed instructions about its location."

"And so you gave instructions to Kenneth Park about how to find it."

Pastor Jeong nodded. "Yes. We have received two emails from him in the past three months. He said that it almost cost him his life, but that the teacup is safe in his possession. But now—"

"He's stuck."

The minister nodded. "He cannot leave the country."

"So where do I come in?" said Ainsley. "I can't just walk around North Korea looking for this man."

"No, Miss Walker," the minister said, an odd twinkle in his eye, "but you can run around."

"What do you mean?"

"Kenneth Park is going to hand you the onyx teacup."

"How?"

"While you are running the marathon."

CHAPTER NINE

Ainsley rocketed out of her chair. "This is a joke, right?"

Placing one hand on her shoulder, the minister gently guided Ainsley back down to her seat.

"It's not a joke," he said. "We have a plan."

"But—"

Pastor Jeong was standing over her now. "Miss Walker, listen to me. In North Korea, nobody has freedom."

"Yes, I know—"

He continued. "You cannot move on your own or speak to the people. You can only enter with a licensed tour group, and all tour groups are controlled by the regime. You only see what the regime wants you to see."

"So it's impossible to meet him."

"Almost, but not quite. At the Mangyongdae Prize International Marathon, the spectators stand along the streets of Pyongyang to watch the runners. It's the only time that an outsider can interact with the people, even for a few seconds."

Ainsley noticed that the congregants were hanging on

every word that she said. She also noticed that the men present all held envelopes in their hands.

She was starting to understand. "And so during this marathon—"

"—you will run past Kenneth Park. He will hand you the treasure as you go by. And then, after you finish the race, you will come back to the United States."

"With the onyx teacup."

"Exactly."

Ainsley sat back in her chair. "So it's really that simple."

"We think so."

Ainsley thought about the task. It would be like passing a baton. And now the minister's questions at the first meeting made sense. She looked at her hands. They were big enough, her fingers long enough, to carry a small teacup.

Pastor Jeong nodded to the young man at the projector, who brought over a folding table and placed it front of Ainsley. The minister placed the contracts on the table and laid a pen alongside them. She could tell that this was showmanship for the congregation.

"You have read the contract?" he said.

"Yes."

"It's satisfactory?"

She nodded. "I think so."

"Do you have any other questions?"

Ainsley thought about it. "Should I dye my hair black?"

The minister smiled and shook his head no. "It's impossible to blend in. Better to stay yourself."

Ainsley frowned. She'd been hoping for a reason to change her look.

"To show our appreciation, this church has taken up a collection for you." Pastor Jeong swept a hand towards the congregation. "All of our families have agreed to contribute. They are donating according to their ability." He looked at

Ainsley. "Please understand—this is in addition to your fee in the contract."

A bonus. The minister knew that this was a dog of an assignment, and this was his congregation's way of sweetening the pot. She wondered how many other people like her had turned down this job.

Meanwhile, the fathers of each family stood up, shuffled down the aisle, and handed their envelopes to the minister.

One by one, Pastor Jeong opened each envelope and counted the bills inside. Ainsley watched the pile grow as he recorded each total. Then he put the cash in a pile next to the contracts.

"Seven hundred and sixteen dollars and forty-five cents."

Ainsley was distracted by the last part of the number. Forty-five cents? Which family was so broke that they were scraping together coins to pay her?

Then the weight of this assignment struck her like an anvil on the head. The people who made up this small congregation—struggling immigrants, probably living in dirty apartments, picking at bare meals beneath bare lightbulbs, trying to make better lives for their children—were willing to part with what little money they had in order to save their church.

They were depending on Ainsley.

She bowed her head. This was different than a rich person sending her off on a lark. This job carried actual moral weight.

Pastor Jeong cleared his throat. "What will you do, Miss Walker?"

She lifted her head, straightened her shoulders, and stared ahead. She felt the answer rising within her.

"I accept," she said.

Ainsley picked up the pen and scrawled her name on both contracts.

The congregation rose to their feet and applauded. For the next half hour, while Ainsley shook hands, hugged children, and pretended to understand their best wishes, she felt an oddly heavy sensation resting between her shoulder blades.

It was a feeling of responsibility.

CHAPTER TEN

A week later, Ainsley chewed on her cuticle while she stared at the flashcard. Printed on the card was a Korean letter.

Holding the card was Daniel Cho. A pair of cappuccinos rested on the table between them. It was Saturday morning, and they had met at a café for a tutoring session in the Korean language.

"Name the letter," said Daniel.

"I can't remember," she replied.

"I thought you said you studied this week."

"I have."

Ainsley's finger itched the black knee brace strapped around her left leg. She'd been running seventeen kilometers day for the last three days, all on concrete. Now she was paying the price.

She stared at the card. "I really can't remember."

"Tell me the rule for Korean characters."

Ainsley sighed. "The characters are drawn in the shape of your mouth when you say them."

"And what shape is this?"

"*Mu*."

"No. It's *bu*."

"Same difference."

"It's the difference between a cow and a hammer."

"Daniel, I'm American."

He grew annoyed. "I'm American too—I was born here. I learned this language by going to Korean school every Saturday morning for four years."

"But this isn't how I learn languages," she said. "I have to speak to people."

"That's not going to happen," Daniel replied. "Your five days in North Korea are going to be so closely monitored that you're going to have to ask permission to take a crap."

Ainsley held up a finger. "Excuse me, women don't do that. We use the toilet."

"Call it what you want. Your only moment of freedom will be during the race."

She thought about it. "I don't know why Pastor Jeong asked me to learn this language anyways."

The young lawyer glanced at her. "Because you never know what might happen."

"He told me that nothing weird is going to happen."

The young lawyer looked at her skeptically. "Sure, until it does. North Korea is unpredictable. They'll get a wild hair for some tourist and yank him off an airplane and make an international announcement about his anti-regime crimes. Then he spends the next six years of his life in a concentration camp in the mountains."

Using her stirrer to slice across the cappuccino foam, Ainsley felt a moment of blissful belonging in the coffee shop. The college student ignoring her open textbook in favor of something incredible on her phone. The old man reading that morning's newspaper, clearly savoring the feel of a newspaper in his fingertips. The barista wiping down the espresso machine.

It was an ordinary place, one that she would've resisted in the past. Ainsley thought back to her own life. When she was younger, and more of a bomb thrower, she would've inwardly railed against the ignorant people here, the ones who went slouching about their lives in a warm bubble of ignorance and solipsism.

Today, however, she wasn't feeling like that at all. The warm scent, the wooden walls, the tattooed baristas—all of them felt strangely comforting.

"Okay," she said, "let's try Korean again."

"Hangeul."

"What's that?"

Daniel sipped his coffee. "The correct word for the Korean language. It was invented five hundred years ago by a king who copied Chinese characters to create a new alphabet."

"That's weird."

"Why?"

"One person invented an entire language?"

"It's not that weird. Especially if you know anything else about Korea."

"I do."

"How?"

"I told you I've been studying."

"All right," said Daniel, "tell me something about Korea."

"Ask me."

He threw his hands into the air. "I don't know. Tell me about the war."

"Which war?"

"To Koreans, there's only been one war."

"Sure."

Ainsley found herself describing the history of the Korean War. Begun by aggressive communists in the north following World War II, resisted by forces in the south, the conflict had swept back and forth over the peninsula like a rolling pin across cookie dough. The U.S. had finally entered the fray by arriving at the southernmost tip of the peninsula, at Busan, and helped the southerners push the communists back. In 1953, the two sides agreed to stop fighting. They settled their differences by creating the demilitarized zone, better known as the DMZ, along the 38th parallel.

That was more than half a century ago. Since then, the two nations had diverged but maintained a zero-sum relationship. As the South has become more prosperous, the North has become more impoverished. The South is the economic pride of the peninsula; the North, its political shame.

Daniel interrupted her. "Ainsley?"

"What?"

"You've been studying," he said, "but let's focus on what's important. Can you order a coffee in Korean?"

His eyes held hers. That was important. She couldn't live without coffee.

Thinking hard, Ainsley finally found the answer. "*Kapuchino han jan ju se yo.*"

Daniel sat back in his chair, studying her. "You are something else."

"Why?"

"That sounded great. It was formal, and with no accent."

Ainsley shrugged. "I guess I do better when I really care about what I'm saying." She reached into her purse. "I have to go. How much do I owe you for your help?"

"It's on me."

"Are you sure?"

Daniel nodded. "Just come home safe, Ainsley."

CHAPTER ELEVEN

With an old towel wrapped around her head, Ainsley stared at her closet in utter confusion.

Packing was proving to be harder than it appeared.

Much easier was the dye job that she'd just finished. Pastor Jeong had advised against it, but he wouldn't be the one traveling to this godforsaken country. It was bad enough that Ainsley was tall. She didn't need hair color to set her apart even more.

She peered at her rack of clothing. Everybody knew what type of clothing to bring on vacation to Europe, Africa, South America. Even the Middle East had dress codes to be followed.

North Korea, on the other hand, was a blank. What kind of outfits did a person bring on a trip to the world's most isolated nation? Kimonos? Military blazers? Levi's 501 blues? Formal gowns? Burlap sacks? Ainsley honestly had no idea.

The only items that she knew for sure to bring were related to the marathon. She pulled open a drawer and dumped its contents onto her bed. Her pink-and-white running shoes. A black long-sleeved running top. A blue short-sleeved running top. Charcoal gray running pants with anti-chafe, flat-locking seams. All pieces that she'd been using for the last two months.

Then Ainsley looked at her luggage. First was her best piece, a creamy beige beauty on rollers, with leather fringe. She ruled it out immediately. Behind that suitcase was a black brocade number on rollers with an extendable handle and extra reinforcements on the sides. She scrunched up her nose. That wouldn't do either—too many frills.

There was only one choice left.

Her athletic duffel bag.

Ainsley pulled it out and crammed all the running clothes inside. Then she went to her closet, shut her eyes, and began pulling random items from the hangers. Tops, pants, sweaters. She stuffed it all into the duffel bag without looking. Then, when she was done, she zipped up the bag and threw it onto the floor and stood over it, hands on hips.

That was how you packed for a trip to North Korea.

The doorbell sounded. Ainsley went over and looked through the peephole.

It was Pastor Jeong.

———

Ainsley opened the door, the surprise evident on her face. "Were we supposed to meet tonight?"

"No," he said, "this is a surprise visit. May I come in?"

"Sure."

She moved aside, and the minister stepped into her apartment and removed his shoes. She noticed that he wore slip-on loafers, which made the process easier. Then he surveyed the interior of the apartment. From his hand hung two plastic shopping bags.

Ainsley stood near the door, embarrassed by the towel around her head. "Is there a problem?"

"No," he said, "we are pleased with your progress. Especially in the language."

"Daniel Cho has been helpful."

"He says that you have natural ability."

Ainsley had heard that before. She'd never had much trouble picking up foreign tongues, especially the basic hundred words and phrases that every traveler needs.

"Did you get the registration confirmation?" she said.

"Yes," he said. "They have you down for the half marathon."

"Good," she replied. "I don't think I can run a full one."

The minister settled himself at her kitchen table. "But there is one part of the assignment that we need to address before you leave."

"What is it?"

He gestured for her to sit. She pulled out the other chair.

"It's the onyx itself."

"Why?"

"The onyx teacup is a minor national treasure," he said, "and the regime is very protective of its art. They have protected their celadon pottery from theft for many years."

Ainsley admitted that the idea of exiting a country with one of its prized gemstones in her suitcase had already struck her as a bit naïve. Every nation had rules protecting its treasures, and North Korea had more rules than most.

"So you're saying that customs officials are going to look through all my items?"

The minister nodded. "Most definitely. And this is how we fix that problem." He handed a shopping bag to her.

"Look inside," he said.

Ainsley peeked in the bag. Inside were several packages of modeling clay. "I don't understand."

The minister explained patiently. "After you get the onyx teacup, you're going to cover it in clay, carve a design in the side, and then tell them that you bought it at a private market."

Ainsley was starting to understand. "So that at customs—"

"They let you take it out."

"Because it looks like an ordinary unfired teacup."

He nodded. "Yes, that's it."

The scheme sounded plausible to Ainsley, except for one thing. "There are private markets in Pyongyang? I thought the regime controlled everything."

"The situation is changing," Pastor Jeong said. "The markets have been growing for the last few years, and the regime pretends not to notice."

Ainsley raised an eyebrow. That was remarkable—a bit of private enterprise in the world's most totalitarian system.

She counted the packets of clay. There were over twenty. "Why did you buy so many?"

"So that you can practice. Here." The minister lifted the second plastic bag. It clinked as he handed it over. "These are about twenty teacups for practice. The congregation took up a collection for you."

"I'll work on it tonight," Ainsley replied, "I promise."

"The congregation also sends prayers that you successfully accomplish your task."

"Tell them I appreciate their thoughts."

Pastor Jeong stood up and went back to the front door and slipped on his shoes. "There is one more thing."

"What?"

"You dyed your hair."

He pointed to her shoulder. Ainsley realized that one piece of her newly dark hair had fallen out of the towel and tumbled onto her shoulders.

"I told you to keep in natural," he continued, "because the North Korean immigration may wonder why you changed the color. Now you have given them a reason to be suspicious of you."

Ainsley was struck speechless. She hadn't thought of that.

"I'm sorry," she finally said.

"Miss Walker, please follow our plan. This way, you don't get in trouble." He offered a tight smile. "Good luck."

Pastor Jeong walked out of the door. When he was gone, Ainsley let out a relieved breath.

From now on, she would follow his instructions.

CHAPTER TWELVE

Seated in a chair at the airport, Ainsley watched the line of passengers shuffle towards the gate, boarding tickets in hand.

It was time for her flight. American Airlines Flight 1067 to Beijing. The boarding pass lay hot inside her coat pocket. From China, she was scheduled to catch a connecting flight to Pyongyang. It was the only way for an American to get to North Korea.

But Ainsley couldn't make herself join the line.

A small voice that dwelled in the depths of her soul was speaking up. It was the voice of self-preservation.

Ainsley heard her stomach growl. If she got on that flight, it was going to have to get used to the deprivation. North Korea wasn't exactly a culinary destination.

Then again, skipping dinner last night hadn't helped. She'd been too immersed in a binge-reading session to notice the minute hand sweeping around the clock face.

The topic of choice had been the Hermit Kingdom. What she had learned had scared her.

Clicking open one of the virtual stack of e-books on her tablet, she'd first read about the history of the Korean peninsula. For almost two thousand years, it'd always considered itself the shrimp between two whales, China and Japan, both of which had taken turns trying to dominate the peninsula. The most recent occupation had been from 1910 to 1945, when Japanese imperialists had subjugated, tortured, and killed hundreds of thousands of Koreans. The starvation had been so bad that, even today, very old Korean people still greet one another with the phrase *Have you eaten rice today?*

It wasn't out of politeness. They were trying to assess who was going to live, and who was going to die.

Then World War II had blown apart the Japanese empire, and the Korean peninsula had found itself suddenly emancipated, but vulnerable. The Soviet Union noticed. Like the bad boy sidling alongside the new divorcée, the Reds swaggered into the northern part of the Korean peninsula, whispering sweet nothings into the lady's ear. The United States had quickly run to the lady's other ear.

Soon the north had fallen for the communists, and the south had fallen for the capitalists.

The leader of the Communist Party was the cherub-faced young man known as Kim Il-Sung. Though three generations of intense propaganda have since painted him as a divine spirit made flesh, one important fact has often been overlooked.

Kim Il-Sung wasn't from Korea.

He'd been raised in northern China, where his family had fled to escape the Japanese. There are even credible rumors that he grew up speaking Mandarin Chinese. If true, that fact would place him squarely in the great tradition of outsider tyrants, ranging from Napoleon (who came from Corsica to rule France) to Stalin (who came from Georgia to rule the Soviet Union).

Ainsley knew how that story ended. She skipped past the

story of the Korean War to the establishment of the North Korean state.

Kim Il-Sung had begun a policy of self-determination known as *juche*, which roughly translates to "self-reliance". It's never been made clear exactly what it represents, but what is certain is that, over time, this ideology pushed North Korea into isolation. It receded even further after Kim's death in 1994, when the country faced the worst two years of its entire history.

The famine.

Outsiders know almost nothing about the particular horrors that gripped the country during the late nineteen-nineties. Experts only know a little more. Most estimate two to three million dead, or nearly ten percent of the entire population. The regime was partly to blame, since it controlled all agriculture. It had also ignored the ancient agricultural technique of terracing.

Dumbfounded, Ainsley read that part twice. In its infinite ignorance, the Kim regime had decided to plant crops directly on the sides of mountains, without leveling the earth. This practice had disturbed the topsoil so much that, after a strong rain, the crops had slid straight down the slopes of the mountains and into the rivers. This denuded the mountains. The arable soil was gone forever, the rivers choked to death.

That's when the starving had really begun.

The elites in Pyongyang got their rations, as did the military, and most of the middle class. But rural peasants and residents of farflung northern cities saw their lives transformed into horror shows. It went like this: Desperate for calories, the families began to kill and eat their livestock. After the livestock had been slaughtered, they looked to their government rations of corn gruel, which barely covered half of an average person's daily requirements. After they had run out of corn gruel, they foraged for wild dandelions and pounded acorns into a gelatinous mush. When the herbs had gone out of season, they pulled bark off the trees to make soup. After the trees had been stripped bare, they pulled the wallpaper paste off their own walls or picked corn kernels out of animal shit.

The most desperate resorted to the most extreme measures. The less said, the better.

Middle-aged women were most likely to survive the famine. The least likely were anybody with a high calorie requirement, such as children under age five and male laborers. Most importantly, this famine had weakened the regime, which tried to put a happy face on the crisis with billboards announcing *Let's Eat Two Meals A Day*.

Ainsley thought about that. When a person has watched her family and friends wither away and die of malnutrition, there wasn't any propaganda that would make her believe in the system again.

Since then, the regime had passed to Kim Il-Sung's son, and then grandson, both of whom continued to blackmail the rest of the world for food. *Give us rice, and we won't use our nuclear weapons*. It was anyone's guess as to how much longer this bizarre arrangement was going to last. China and South Korea, both neighbors, have propped the regime for one very cynical reason—sending bags of rice was easier than dealing with twenty million starving people pouring across the border.

Still, everyone knew that the regime was standing with fingers in the dyke. It couldn't last forever.

And Ainsley was flying into the cold heart of the country.

"Last call, American Airlines flight ten sixty-seven to Beijing, last call for boarding," said the gate agent, the microphone pressed sideways against his mouth.

Sighing, Ainsley got to her feet, slung her carry-on over her shoulder, and joined the rear of the line. A moment later, she handed her boarding pass to the gate agent, received the stub in return, and moved down the long walkway.

She was the last person in line. Ahead, seventy people waited patiently to duck their heads and step onto the airbus for the transpacific flight.

She felt her phone vibrate in her hand. She looked at the screen. It was a text message from Daniel Cho:

I didn't want to tell you before you left because I thought it might spook you out but if something goes weird or whatever in Pyongyang, the only way to escape the country is to bribe your way to the Yalu River and then cross illegally into China. So yeah good luck lol

Ainsley felt the panic rising. He really hadn't needed to tell her that. Then her phone vibrated again. His second message:

I've told some of my Korean friends about you btw and they're like srsly be careful and come back safe

That did it. She wasn't going to leave. There was still time to turn back.

Ainsley jammed her phone back into her pocket. She pivoted on her heel and began walking back towards the gate.

Ahead, the gate agent slammed the door shut.

Breaking into a run, Ainsley reached the door a moment later. It was locked. Through the porthole, she could see the agent already walking away down the concourse. Ainsley pounded on the glass with her fist.

"Let me out!" she shouted.

He couldn't hear her. Nobody could.

Ainsley calmed herself down. Then she turned and trudged back down the gangplank, towards the airplane.

Towards North Korea.

CHAPTER THIRTEEN

Cupping her hands on the window of the Air China jet, she peered down at the capital of North Korea.

Pyongyang.

From the sky, it seemed like a city of gray—gray avenues, gray buildings, gray monuments, gray air. She wondered if it would be any different on the ground.

The airplane touched down and taxied to a stop. As the flight attendants opened the door, the passengers stood up. Behind her were a group of thin Caucasians who looked visibly nervous. Ainsley guessed that they were running the marathon too.

Outside the airplane, they were ushered down a steep mobile staircase to the ground. Ainsley noticed the difference in the air. It smelled metallic and sharp, like a dangerous factory.

The passengers followed a walkway across the tarmac and entered the customs gate. Three severe agents stood behind three severe desks. They were looking at passports.

Ainsley stood there, waiting in line, a little weak at the knees from the trip. To the right was a room sealed behind a pane of glass. She their suitcases were being neatly assembled in a line on a long stainless steel table. Her duffel bag was in the middle of the queue.

She tried not to snicker. They weren't going to find anything incriminating in her luggage. She doubted that lip balm constituted a threat to the regime.

At last she arrived at the desk. Wordlessly, she handed over her passport. The woman behind the counter had the face of an assassin. She opened the booklet and held it up in the air. Her cold black eyes flipped back and forth between the photo and Ainsley.

Then she barked something in Korean.

Ainsley was startled. Pastor Jeong had warned her that the North Korean accent was harsh, but she was unprepared for this. It sounded like the vicious barking a person makes when in physical pain. The spirit was everything.

Ainsley struggled for a response. The agent pointed to her hair and barked the same thing.

Ah. It was about the dye job. Ainsley had prepared for this moment. "*Jega baggutseopnida*," she said. In English: *I changed it*.

That seemed to satisfy the agent. Then she said, "*Han fone*."

Ainsley didn't understand. "*Dasi?*" Again?

"*Han fone*."

The agent stuck out her thumb and her pinky and held it up to the side of her face.

Then Ainsley understood. *Han fone* was borrowed from English. It meant *mobile phone*.

Ainsley dug into her bag and lifted her phone. The agent gestured for it. Ainsley handed it over and watched as the woman dropped it inside a white plastic bag, wrapped it in an official-looking black tape, and then sealed it shut with a pool of old-fashioned red wax. The agent scrawled some words on the outside of the package, then handed it back.

The intent was clear: This was not to be used. If Ainsley cracked open the seal, there'd be hell to pay upon exit.

Then the agent stamped her passport, handed it back, and motioned for the next person.

Moving along, Ainsley found herself in a vast room that looked as though it'd been built in the nineteen-sixties. It was mostly empty except for the crowd of travelers milling around a row of stanchions. She guessed that was where the luggage would be released.

She scanned the room, looking for the tour guide who was supposed to be greeting her. There: a pudgy man near a pillar, wearing a black suit with gold epaulets. On his face were a pair of epic jowls and an expression of serene self-satisfaction. In his hands was a sign that read Mangyongdae Prize International Marathon.

Ainsley headed for the man, trying to walk casually. She noticed that the other foreigners from the plane were headed towards him as well.

Soon the group had circled around him. The man cleared his throat. "Welcome to the Democratic People's Republic of Korea. Please tell me your names."

Ainsley tried not to smirk. The Democratic People's Republic of Korea, or DPRK for short, was a ridiculous name. There had been no trace of democracy here for over half a century.

One by one, the people around the circle offered their names. Gemma. Dean. Hans. Israel.

The official turned to Ainsley. "And your name, please." She noticed that he spoke with a distinct Australian accent.

"Ainsley Walker."

He nodded, checked her name off the list. "Welcome again, contestants," he said. "My name is Kyung-hee Dae. I am your official escort to the Mangyongdae Prize International Marathon. You may have noticed that I speak English. Many tourists ask me, why I speak such very good English."

It wasn't that good, thought Ainsley, but better than expected.

"Hollywood movies?" someone said.

"It is forbidden to watch Western movies in this country," he answered. "No, I learned it at Pyongyang University. Does that surprise you? After that, however, I studied in Australia for a year. If you were wondering a question, yes, I have eaten kangaroo—but I still prefer kimchi."

That was evidently a punchline, because he paused, waiting for laughter. He'd clearly delivered this little spiel before. A half-hearted chuckle sounded from the back of the group.

Satisfied, Kyung-hee continued: "Because I have experienced life outside of North Korea, I can say that you will be very surprised at how wonderful life is inside of North Korea during your vacation."

He looked Ainsley for a response, probably because she was standing closest to him. She mustered up the best smile she could find and pasted it to her face.

"I'm looking forward to it," she said.

The translator nodded. "Again, my name is Kyung-hee. This is Kyung-joon."

He made a quick gesture. Ainsley turned and saw another escort standing nearby, watching them. This was a fitter man with a hawkish look in his eyes, wearing the same black suit.

"Together we will answer all of your questions about the country. We will also help you prepare for the race." Then he added: "If we're ready to go, the coach is waiting outside. There is an orientation and welcome party in the hotel conference room at four o'clock to discuss the schedule for the week."

Ainsley raised her hand. "What about our luggage?"

"It will be delivered to the hotel later today."

She felt the implication hanging in the air. "You're saying it will be searched."

"Yes."

A moment later, as they were being escorted towards the pickup area, she glanced back at the luggage room. A guard in an olive military uniform with red-and-yellow patches on the collar was using a massive pair of pliers to wrench the zipper off an expensive Louis Vuitton suitcase.

Ainsley grimaced. That was why she'd left the good bags at home.

CHAPTER FOURTEEN

At four o'clock that afternoon, Ainsley squinted her eyes at the buttons on the elevator. They read G, 2, 3, 4, and 6.

There was no fifth floor.

She was in the Yanggakdo International Hotel, a forty-seven-story beast a couple of kilometers southeast of downtown Pyongyang. The hotel's exterior was unwelcoming—a sheer silver wall, a brutal and merciless modern design. It'd been built in the mid-nineties by a French company and was the second-tallest building in the country. The tallest was an unfinished 105-story pyramid hotel, an eyesore on the skyline that had been under occasional construction for more than thirty years.

However, the building was located on an island in the middle of the river. It was surrounded by manicured grounds and walking paths. Ainsley had been surprised at the beauty of the site. However, the only entry onto the island was a bridge, which was heavily gated. A guard checked every vehicle that passed in and out.

Visitors called it Alcatraz.

Ainsley's room had proven to be surprisingly plush. It had

good bedding and a stiff white club chair and small desk. Another surprise was the fact that she had been given a roommate, who was currently standing next to her in the elevator.

Hanna.

Taller than most men, with a head of thinning blonde hair, Hanna was a divorced television executive from Amsterdam. She'd started running marathons for fun more than a decade earlier. She'd said that this was her fifteenth.

"Hanna," said Ainsley, "have you noticed that there's no fifth floor?"

The Dutchwoman shook her head. "There is one, but I was told that we are not allowed to enter it."

"Why?"

"I don't know. Maybe it is where the government keeps all of its, how do you say, surveillance equipment?"

That made sense. Onsite, the regime could more effectively monitor the international visitors. She'd even caught herself wondering if the mirror in their bathroom happened to be two-way.

"Maybe."

"I would like to see the fifth floor," said her roommate. "There must be a stairway."

Ainsley shook her head. "No, I wouldn't try to go there."

The elevator doors opened, and the two women strode across the wide marble lobby. The ceiling was tilted at a rakish angle, the brass accents minimalist. Everything felt unexpectedly modern. It would be easy for Ainsley to let down her guard here.

To forget the danger that lay off the island.

"I have to ask the staff a question," said Hanna.

Ainsley shrugged. She had nowhere to be.

They approached the front desk, which was a long marble counter well-lit by recessed lights. The clerk, a young woman with short black bangs, stood behind a computer monitor. She had an attractive bow-shaped mouth and a button nose.

"Hello," said Hanna, "I had a second bag. Can you tell me where it is?"

"What is your name?" said the girl. She spoke English, but her accent was guttural. It was disconcerting to hear such an inelegant voice coming from a pretty face.

"Hanna Hendriks. Room 1713."

The girl picked at the keyboard, looked at the screen, and pivoted on one heel. Ainsley watched her walk away. She carried herself with a controlled gait, spine erect. It seemed that the girl had been chosen to interact with international guests as much for her appearance as for her competence in English.

The girl returned from the back room. "The bag is here, but it's not available yet."

Hanna crinkled her brow. "What do you mean?"

"We will deliver it to your room."

The Dutchwoman turned away, frustrated. "These people."

"What's in the bag?" said Ainsley.

"Something important."

"Tell me."

The woman grinned. "You'll see."

Together they ascended the short circular marble staircase to the mezzanine level, where they found the conference room. A few hundred people had assembled for the briefing. Ainsley and Hanna took a couple of seats and waited for the orientation to begin.

Kyung-hee emerged onto the low dais, took the podium, and spoke into the microphone. He welcomed everybody. Today was Monday, and he laid out the schedule for the next week. There would be a group training run tomorrow, Tuesday. Then a city trip all day Wednesday, and a second training run on Thursday. On Friday was the sponsored trip to the demilitarized zone.

Saturday was the marathon.

Ainsley grew bored with the presentation. The running would be decent, but she didn't relish the idea of being led by the nose around Pyongyang, not any more than she had to be. She listened to him rattle off all the sights. The Arch of Triumph, designed to dwarf the one in Paris. The Juche Tower. The Grand People's Study House, the central library.

She just didn't have patience for any of it. Ainsley couldn't pretend that this was a nice place to visit. She wished there was a way to fast-forward to Saturday, grab the onyx teacup from Kenneth Park, and sprint directly to the airport.

Her attention drifted back into the presentation. A new person was at the microphone, an Asian-American in his mid-twenties.

"Hanna," whispered Ainsley, "I wasn't listening—who is this guy?

"His name is Eugene," the Dutchwoman replied. "I don't know his last name. He went to Harvard and now runs a nonprofit that trains North Koreans in modern management practices."

Ainsley wondered how successful that could be in a centrally-controlled communist economy. "Why are we listening to him?"

"Because he's telling us how to behave here."

Ainsley forced herself to tune in. Eugene was explaining rules of photography, which boiled down to pretty much no photos of anything, period. He explained how 3G mobile used to be available to foreigners before the government banned it. How North Koreans wealthy enough to own smart phones still are forbidden from visiting international websites or making international calls or sending international text messages. How the citizens are allowed to swap music, pictures, and games with one another. That was a surprise.

Then he moved onto dress code. Technically, women weren't allowed to wear pants. Then he quickly added that you could probably get away with it, unless you were to run into an anti-pants patrol, but fortunately those groups only worked in certain neighborhoods at certain times of the day. He went also explained that women were also technically banned from riding bicycles.

By now, Ainsley was rapt, as was everybody in the room. Only citizens deemed loyal to the regime were allowed to live in the capital, Eugene said, mostly because it's the only city that foreigners are allowed to visit. Preference was also given to residents who were attractive.

Finally he paused for a drink of water. "Are there any questions?"

One woman raised her hand. "Where do you live, Eugene?"

"All of us NGOs live in the diplomatic compound. It's nice, I guess. I mean, there's a bar on the corner where you can drink beer."

Laughter. Another hand rose. "Do you have a girlfriend here?"

Eugene looked uneasy. "No. But not for lack of trying. Let's just say that the girls here in the capital aren't, um, interested in dating Americans."

Another person stood up. "Do you have a car?"

"Sure."

"Really?"

He nodded. "Yeah. I mean, I drove here today."

"There's nobody monitoring you?"

"Not as far as I know," Eugene replied. "There's a liaison officer who sorts out whatever I need with the bureaucracy, but he's not like a guard. Inside Pyongyang, I move around normally, though there's a few places I can't go. The problems only really start when you want to leave the city. Nobody is allowed to go out into the country without a permit."

Ainsley realized how little she knew about daily life in this country. All she ever heard about from the headlines were the latest obnoxious public saber-rattling that the regime was making. Over the years it had publicly called America an empire of devils, a group of Satan, and a toothless wolf. It had compared South Korean President Park Geun-Hye to a blabbering peasant woman, and U.S. President Barack Obama to a monkey in a tropical forest.

But the regime didn't speak for the people, who probably carried on as best they could. Ainsley imagined that there were good North Koreans, bad North Koreans, and a whole lot of ordinary North Koreans who could be tipped either way. But she honestly didn't care enough to find out. She just wanted to leave the country as soon as possible.

Polite applause as Eugene stepped off the dais, and Kyung-hee bounded back up to the microphone. "To welcome you on your first night in the Democratic People's Republic of Korea, the restaurant on the forty-seventh floor has prepared a special dinner for you."

He gestured to the long accordion wall on one side of the room. It was pulled back by a pair of workers, revealing a long buffet table loaded with crabs, noodles, rice, vegetables, and other traditional Korean foods.

"Please form a line on the left," he said. "Enjoy."

Soon, everybody was out of their seats and lining up for plates. Ainsley joined Hanna near the front, and a moment later she was scooping *chap chae*, or glass noodles, onto her plate.

"This is unbelievable," said her roommate, gesturing to the spread. "I hope everybody in the country eats like this."

"They don't," Ainsley replied. "The regime is laying out the red carpet for us."

Then Ainsley spotted Eugene, the young speaker. He was a few steps away, loading his plate with bulgogi and rice.

She approached him and introduced herself. "I loved your talk."

"Thank you," he said, shaking her hand. "They always ask me to do it because they know that I can communicate with Westerners better than they can. But I still have to watch what I say."

"Do you think we could talk privately?"

"Maybe," he said. Then looked Ainsley up and down, and she realized that he'd misinterpreted her intention.

"About the regime," she added.

He shook his head. "I'd rather not."

"Never?"

He made a fifty-fifty gesture with his hands. "It's dangerous." He regarded Ainsley with a critical eye. "I don't get it. Do you want to get in trouble? I mean, just run the marathon."

Ainsley decided to come clean. "Eugene, I'm actually here for another reason."

She took him by the arm and pulled him away from the people around the buffet. Lowering her voice, she quickly explained her assignment to recover the onyx teacup. He set down his plate and listened intently.

When she'd finished, he appeared to be a little shaken. "You're playing with fire."

"You think so?"

"They'll be watching the racecourse. Cameras, maybe personnel."

"A quick high-five. That's it. No way they can see that. And the teacup is small enough to fit in my palm."

"True." He thought for a moment. "What's your name again?"

"Ainsley Walker."

"Ainsley, I'm giving you my phone number. We should get together this week so I can dissuade you from doing this."

Eugene pulled a paper from his pocket and jotted down his number and handed it to her. "See the last digit?"

"Yeah, it's a seven."

"Change it to a zero when you dial. I don't want this number falling into the wrong hands."

Ainsley understood what he meant. You couldn't be too careful here.

"Thank you," she said.

"Call me," he said. "I'm serious. I'll show you around Pyongyang."

Eugene grinned, then walked off back towards the buffet. Ainsley found herself smiling.

She couldn't blame a lonely guy in North Korea for trying to land some female company.

CHAPTER FIFTEEN

The next morning, Ainsley woke up to the sound of metal scraping on metal.

She lifted her head from the pillow, blinked twice. Sunlight was streaming in through the wide windows. In front of the window, perched on the edge of her chair, her roommate was busy assembling a device. It had three legs and a long cylinder.

"Good morning," said Hanna.

Ainsley rubbed her eyes. "What are you doing?"

"It's a beautiful morning to spy on people."

She mounted the cylinder upon the tripod and swung the narrower end around to her face. Then Ainsley recognized the object.

It was a telescope.

She sat up in bed. A mop of black hair fell onto her face. It frightened her until she realized that it was her own hair. "You brought a telescope to North Korea?"

Hanna adjusted the focus. "Can you believe they let it through?"

"No, I can't. Why would you do that?"

"Simple," answered Hanna. "If they won't let us walk around the city, then I am going to see it from here." She pressed her left eye to the eyepiece and swung the lens around, then stopped. "Incredible. I just found a market."

Ainsley climbed out of bed. "Really? One of those open-air ones?"

"Yes. They're called *jangmadang*."

"They're supposed to be illegal."

"No," she replied, "supposedly the markets are popping up everywhere now."

Ainsley shrugged. "I don't think anybody really knows what's allowed and what's not."

Hanna stepped aside, and Ainsley slid into the chair and lifted her body up to the eyepiece. Her hand adjusted the focus until the image came into clarity. It was a small, dirty square in the city. Ringing the square were about thirty low folding tables. She could make out piles of vegetables, bags of rice, boxes of electronics, and stacks of clothing.

"Isn't it fun to spy on people?" said Hanna. Her face was glowing.

Ainsley admired the telescope. "I seriously can't believe they let this through."

"I wouldn't have cared if they'd confiscated it."

"Why?"

"It belonged to my ex-husband."

Ainsley smiled. She swung the telescope a block to the west and quickly noticed a bright red billboard painted on the side of a gray warehouse. It was a lurid depiction of a sledgehammer smashing into the skull of an American soldier. Blood and brain matter exploded from the back of his head.

Ainsley felt a shiver in her spine.

Below the propaganda was a narrow alley. Ainsley angled the telescope down slightly and saw two black-clad figures standing just inside the entrance. They were locked in an embrace.

She knew that body language, remembered it well. It was teenage love. It made her smile to see it here, in Pyongyang, like a single blossom in an enormous turd.

"We should get dressed," said Hanna. "We're meeting downstairs for the training run in twenty minutes."

———

Twenty minutes later, Ainsley stood in line with forty other runners. They were waiting to board the bus that was going to take them to a training facility for the practice run.

At the doorway of the bus stood Kyung-joon, the escort with the hawkish look. He was holding a clipboard with a roster of competitors.

"Name, please," he said.

"Ainsley Walker." Then she added: "Half marathon."

His finger scrolled down the list until he found her name. "Ain-slee Wokker. You run full mara-ton."

"No, half."

He double-checked the list. "No, you run full mara-ton."

"But I signed up for the half."

"No."

Ainsley grew frustrated with his brusque manner. "Can you change it?"

He frowned stiffly. "Is not possible. Mara-ton is Sat-uh-day. No time. You run full mara-ton."

That was the third time he'd said that. Ainsley decided to plead her case. "Is there anybody else that I can talk to?"

He stared at her. "You run full mara-ton."

Grumbling to herself, Ainsley climbed on board the bus and found a seat next to Hanna.

"What happened?" she said.

"I'm supposed to run the half marathon, but they've got me registered for the full marathon. He won't change it."

The Dutchwoman shrugged. "Maybe you could bribe them."

Ainsley shook her head. "That would never work."

"I've travelled the world for my job. It's how business gets done outside of developed countries."

As the bus driver started the engine, Ainsley looked out the window and thought about that.

CHAPTER SIXTEEN

Ainsley milled around at the outside edge of the tour group, waiting for the dance squad to begin their choreography.

She was utterly bored.

It was Wednesday, and they were in the middle of the daylong city tour. At the moment, they were standing at the edge of an awful Soviet-style public square.

Arranged on the square were nearly a hundred North Korean dancers in tight formation, spaced equally apart. The men wore short white-sleeved shirts and ties, the women colorful polyester dresses. Their arms were held stiffly at their sides, their faces hard and expressionless.

Ainsley glanced at Hanna. The tall Dutchwoman watched the scene with bright, shining eyes.

"Isn't this interesting?" she said.

"Not really."

"We get to meet the people."

"No," corrected Ainsley, "you get to admire their choreography routine."

"Maybe we can talk to them."

Ainsley sighed. "Look at their expressions. They're just

shilling for the tourists. They don't want to be here any more than we do."

"I want to be here," replied the Dutchwoman.

Ainsley grew sullen. "Then maybe you're just a better person than me."

At that moment, from the audio speakers that ringed the square, there came the sound of a sappy romantic song. The strings were weepy, the rhythm waltz-like. To Ainsley's ears, it sounded ridiculously outdated, like something Lawrence Welk would've recorded. That made sense. The regime had officially banned all expressions of Western culture sixty years earlier. The musical taste of North Koreans hadn't changed in half a century.

On cue, the dancers began to move. They took three awkward steps forward, then three equally awkward steps back. Their arms swooped oddly through the air. They turned on their heels, the women swinging fans, the men performing courtly bows. It looked like a demented Stalinist version of a nineteenth-century formal ball.

Then the group made two simultaneous hops to the right and swept their arms out wide like an airplane. Two hops to the left and the same.

Intricate. Rehearsed.

And totally lifeless.

The event left Ainsley feeling even worse. You couldn't really call this dancing, not if you define dancing as the expression of one's soul through physical movement. There was zero passion on display here.

Along the edge of the square stood a line of officials. One of them, a severe man in the usual olive outfit with red-and-yellow patches at the collar, begin to move through the dancers. He was inspecting them. He swatted one dancer's hand, then pointed at her feet.

Ainsley leaned over. "What do you think the crime was?"

"She fell out of step," answered Hanna. "I saw it happen."

"Horrible."

"Awful."

"Death penalty for sure."

The song mercifully ended, and the performers faced the small crowd of tourists. Ainsley found herself applauding against her will.

As the performers left the square, Kyung-hee stepped up onto a park bench with a microphone in his hand. He pointed to the large statue behind the square. It was a trio of enormous hands holding a hammer, a sickle, and a brush.

"This is the Workers' Party monument," he said. "In Korea, there are many monuments that the people have raised to the spirit of Juche. Building great works to defend our homeland against the aggressive American imperialists. And our lost brothers who have become their puppets."

Ainsley ran her pinky around the inside of her ear. Had she heard that right? Americans were the imperialists? Really? What could North Koreans possibly believe that Americans wanted from their peninsula? Weeds? Empty factories? The U.S. already had plenty of both. True, the U.S. kept a military presence in South Korea, but the South Koreans welcomed it, even paid for the presence. It was undoubtedly true that Americans were cultural imperialists, however, swamping the world with their television and movies and music and books, but North Korea had none of that.

The regime had invented a story, and had been telling it, over and over, for more than sixty years now. It was a depressing truth. If you tell a big enough lie, and keep repeating the lie, people will eventually believe it.

She turned her attention back to Kyung-hee. "And now, the Great Successor will continue the proud task. He has already begun to—"

"Kim Jong-eun is so young," whispered Hanna. "Have you seen him? Twenty-seven when he took power."

"Really?" said Ainsley.

"Yes, I swear it."

"That can't be right."

"Ask him."

Ainsley raised her hand. Kyung-hee stopped talking. "Yes?"

"When was Kim Jong-eun born?" she said.

The tour guide grew suddenly cold. "It is prohibited to ask such questions in Democratic People's Republic of Korea."

Ainsley was confused. "Why?"

Kyung-hee struggled to find a polite answer. His face contorted oddly. An Australian man standing nearby touched her sleeve. "It's because Kim Jong-eun is considered a god."

"You're kidding."

The man shook his head. "It's true. He doesn't have an age, because he wasn't ever born, because he's technically a god."

Ainsley stifled a laugh. Hanna interjected. "But there's a picture of him at boarding school in Switzerland as a boy—"

"The North Korean people haven't seen that picture," said the Australian.

Ainsley struggled to keep her eyes from rolling backwards in her skull.

"May I continue?" said Kyung-hee.

"I'm sorry," said Ainsley. "This man has explained everything to me. I apologize for the question."

As he droned on, Ainsley let her eyes wander around the city. On the other side of the wide, empty boulevard, behind a series of concrete pylons and metal chains, marched a line of schoolchildren. They wore black shorts with white tops and black suspenders and loose red neckerchiefs around their necks. They seemed surprisingly happy. Then again, children could be happy in a prisoner-of-war camp. They didn't know any better.

Then she noticed the four military officers. They had arrived quietly behind the group and were standing at attention. Side by side, arms stiffly behind their backs. She cocked her head, staring at them.

The olive uniforms and the red sashes against gray concrete. It was an arresting image.

Ainsley reached into her bag and pulled out her camera. She held it to her face, pointed it at the group.

She felt a stern presence at her shoulder. "Miss Wokker."

Ainsley's stomach hit her shoes. It was Kyung-joon, and he didn't look pleased. He would never look pleased.

"Yes?" she said.

"Is pro-heebit to photo the military."

His black eyes flicked towards the camera in her hand.

"I'm sorry," she replied.

"Give me."

Ainsley didn't argue. She handed him the camera. His fingers found the memory bank. He swiped through all her photos. She watched him delete three. Then he handed it back to her.

"I'm sorry," she repeated.

"If you continue, you have prob-lem," he warned. "Okay?"

"Loud and clear, boss." She fought the urge to jokingly chuck him in the shoulder.

His eyes searched hers for a moment, as hard and as empty as lumps of coal. Then he walked back to the bus. Ainsley and Hanna exchanged glances but said nothing.

A minute later, the speech ended. As she reboarded the bus, Ainsley walked past Kyung-joon.

His merciless black eyes were still fixated upon her.

CHAPTER SEVENTEEN

When the dish landed with a thud on the placemat, Ainsley's mouth dropped open. This was like no casserole she'd ever seen.

The tour group was sitting at a long table in a restaurant in what passed for the trendy part of the city. Tonight they were scheduled to experience nightlife in Pyongyang, such as it was.

She'd ordered something that was described as savory casserole, according to the translation sheet that accompanied the menu. What had been delivered to her placemat was a black ceramic pot filled with twisty noodles swimming in a weird gray sauce. Stringy bits of green stalks and red peppers dotted the pile. A few brown strips of well-done mystery meat lay atop the dish.

"What is wrong with these people?" she said.

Hanna looked up from her plate of kimchi. The leaves of fermented cabbage dangled from her chopsticks.

"That's going to be a long answer," she replied.

"Look. I ordered a casserole."

Hanna peered into the pot. "It looks more like a stew."

"And this meat? Look. What the hell is it?"

"It's a miracle," said Hanna. "Nobody gets meat in this country. Enjoy."

Ainsley took her spoon in her left hand, her chopsticks in her right, and lifted a twirl of noodles to her mouth. They were oddly pungent and oily. She managed to swallow the mouthful.

Hanna saw her face. "You need the carbohydrates for Saturday."

"But it's disgusting."

"So try the meat."

Ainsley lifted a strip of the mystery meat and placed it in her mouth. She began to chew. It was gamey, stringy, and scorched.

"Oh God, it's even worse."

Hanna smiled. "So did you look at the drinks menu yet?"

"No."

A smile appeared on her face as she handed Ainsley another menu. "Go to the bottom and read the last one. It's incredible."

Ainsley went to the last item on the list. *Seal penis liquor*.

"Can you believe it?"

Ainsley closed the menu and threw down her chopsticks. "This place is horrible. I'm finished."

Hanna's eyes were drawn to something on the other side of the room. "Look, our entertainment has arrived."

Ainsley turned around. Behind her, four tiny young women were walking in a line across the floor. They were dressed in bizarre red plastic skirts and wore yellow plastic flowers in their hair. They looked like animated dolls.

Then Ainsley saw the stage. It had already been set up for the show. A drum kit, guitar amps, microphones.

The girls took the stage and, without any fanfare, began to play. Loudly. One tiny girl bashed the drum kit, another attacked her guitar. A third played the bass guitar. The instrument was so big, and the girl so small, that her left hand literally couldn't reach the top of the neck.

Ainsley listened to the band with passing interest. They were pounding out an extremely simple three-chord rock song. It sounded a lot like surf rock from the early nineteen-fifties. She guessed that this was their stuck-in-time way of welcoming Western tourists.

She looked at her plate. It smelled horrible. She looked at the drummer, her stubby arms pounding relentlessly on the snare drum. She listened the singer caterwauling on the microphone. None of this enjoyable.

It was time for the bathroom.

Ainsley stood up and went to the back of the restaurant, pushed inside the ladies' room, and looked at herself in the small mirror over the sink. Her face looked tight, stressed out. She couldn't relax in this country. Even a day of supposedly pleasant sightseeing carried undercurrents of unpleasant truths.

And then there was the marathon on Saturday. She would be running all of it. That was unthinkable. What kind of security threat would it honestly pose to change her registration? It was their mistake anyways. Then again, Ainsley knew that she was applying Western standards of customer service to a nation that didn't even have a word for customer.

She turned on the hot water and plunged her hands into the stream, scrubbing them with an oddly scented bar of soap. When she finished, she spun around, searching for towels or a hand dryer. There were none.

Instead, she ran her hands down her pants, then opened the door—

—and stumbled into Kyung-hee. The pudgy tour guide was waiting, his arms crossed, against the wall.

"Miss Walker," he said.

"Good evening."

"How are you enjoying dinner?"

"It's different. The meat is weird."

One corner of his mouth lifted in a sad mockery of a smile. "I hear you are signed up for the full marathon."

"Yes, unfortunately."

"I can help you change it."

"Kyung-joon said no changes."

The North Korean escort shrugged, then casually inspected a fingernail. His silence said everything.

Ainsley understood. This was the moment. She reached into her pocket, found a wad of bills, and handed them to her guide. He quickly stuffed them into his pocket without looking.

"How much is it?" he said.

"About thirty dollars US."

The guide grinned. "I will make the change happen. Thank you."

"No, thank you."

As she stepped away, Kyung-hee caught her arm. "One more thing. That meat?"

"Yes."

"It's dog meat."

Ainsley clutched her stomach and turned back into the bathroom.

CHAPTER EIGHTEEN

At nine o'clock the next morning, Ainsley was in the back of the bus again, bouncing down a rutted highway.

This was the Reunification Highway.

Ainsley looked out the window. The surface of this six-lane behemoth certainly could use some reunification. It was pocked with fissures, fractures, and holes. It was totally empty. The tour group had been driving south from Pyongyang for well over an hour and only passed one other vehicle.

She watched, flashing by the window, the lines of weeds that sprouted between the edges of the gray lanes. Then a sign: Seoul 300 km. That was uncharacteristically optimistic. She'd heard that there was a similar freeway on the other side of the border, in South Korea, equally unmaintained, and equally empty.

Ainsley felt something plastic land in her lap. It was a large water bottle. Next to her, Hanna was opening a second one.

"You have to hydrate," she said. "Tomorrow's the big day."

Ainsley unscrewed the bottle and gulped a quarter of it,

then replaced the screw top. "I hope they have a bathroom at the DMZ."

"They will. It's a tourist site."

"It's also an active conflict zone." Ainsley felt her stomach rumble. "The only bright spot this whole week has been when Kyung-hee agreed to change my status."

"What? When did he do that?"

"When I talked to him at that horrible restaurant. I'm running the half-marathon tomorrow."

The Dutchwoman seemed stupefied. "I thought you said that Kyung-joon said it wasn't possible to change."

"That was Kyung-joon. Kyung-hee is more open."

"How did you do that?"

"I paid him."

"You gave him a bribe?"

"Yes."

"Kyung-hee took a bribe from you? Alone?"

"Yes."

A worried look clouded Hanna's face. "That's not good."

"Why not? Remember, you suggested it."

Hanna paused. "Yes, but every country does it differently. Here, they always work in pairs when dealing with foreigners to avoid any improper dealings. You have to bribe both of them."

Ainsley shrugged. "It's his problem."

"It could be your problem."

"How?"

"If he gets caught by the other guy, he'll blame you."

Ainsley felt herself blanch. That scenario hadn't occurred to her. "I'm sure it won't be an issue," she said. "He's just going to change the distance on my registration card."

They both fell silent. Ainsley listened to the hum of tires on the pavement, the murmur of the others' voices around her.

"Can I ask you a question?" said Hanna.

"Sure."

"What are you really doing here?"

Ainsley looked at her. "I'm running the marathon."

Hanna shook her head. "But you hate the marathon. You hate this country. I'm a journalist and more importantly, a woman. I know when someone is lying or withholding the truth."

Ainsley felt miserable. She couldn't avoid the subject forever. "Are you sure you want to hear?"

"Yes."

In a quiet voice, Ainsley explained everything—the church, the onyx teacup, the assignment. The handoff from Kenneth Park. The plan with the clay.

"So you're a gemstone investigator?" said Hanna.

"Yes."

"That's quite a niche." Hanna thought for a moment. "So where are you going to meet this guy?"

"They told me that we come out a tunnel, turn left, and follow the river. He'll be in the spectators on the right."

Hanna lifted an eyebrow. "This sounds very difficult. I hope it works."

Ainsley grew quiet. "Please don't tell anybody."

"Your secret is safe with me. Until we get home."

"What?"

Hanna smiled. "I'm a journalist, Ainsley. This will make a great special—with your cooperation, of course."

Ainsley decided to save that conversation for later.

Eventually the bus pulled off the rutted freeway and moved through a forest, slowing down for a peremptory checkpoint. Ainsley watched the military members wave the bus through.

A second checkpoint came into view, and Kyung-hee stood up at the front of the bus and addressed the group.

"We are going to enter the Joint Security Area at Panmunjom. This visit requires entry into a hostile area and possibility of injury or death as a direct result of enemy action. You are required to sign this paper before we continue."

Several copies of a waiver were handed through the bus. Ainsley read through it. It was from the tour company—not the government—and it was written in English, stating an unequivocal release of the tour company from all potential damages that lay on the other side of this checkpoint.

Ainsley signed her own and handed it to Kyung-hee as he came down the aisle. "Excuse me, when do we get lunch?"

He waved her off. "Not now."

Ainsley sat back, annoyed. Her stomach was still grumbling.

Once all the waivers had been collected, Kyung-hee spoke to the driver. The bus moved past the second checkpoint, and a minute later was parked in a small dirt lot bounded by cement stanchions.

"Please show respect here," said Kyung-hee. "No photos. Keep your shoes and coats on. Don't look at the soldiers in their eyes. Again, no photos."

The tourists quickly disembarked, and Ainsley found herself blinking in the cold light of a cold spring morning.

In front of her was a huge expanse of brown scrubland, dotted with dirt tracks and the occasional bush or tree. It was at least eight hundred meters across. Spaced around the nearest half of the field were thirty North Korean troops. They stood at the ready, rifles gripped in both hands, dressed in the customary olive drab with red sash.

They all faced the other side of the scrubland.

Ainsley squinted. On the distant southern half were stationed another thirty troops, similarly spaced—but they were wearing different clothing. Light gray shirts with dark gray pants. Black helmets with gray bands. Black armbands around their left biceps. They held rifles as well.

Those were South Korean troops.

It was a standoff. It had been going on for generations.

Ainsley felt fear begin its menacing crawl up her spine. Despite the distance between the soldiers, the two sides stood facing their counterparts with utter seriousness. It was clear to her why former U.S. President Bill Clinton had called the DMZ "the scariest place on earth".

Kyung-hee led the group to a position under the edge of the woods, a safe distance away from the soldiers. He began to describe the history of this piece of land. It used to be the village of Panmunjeom, but since that was destroyed in the war, it's simply known as Truce Village. It's the only place along the border where North Korean and South Korean soldiers are allowed to face one another. The two sides occasionally meet for discussions, which sometimes end in gunshots, but each side is prohibited from crossing the line of demarcation into the opposite half of the field. This prohibition began in 1976 with the Axe Murder Incident, in which North Korean troops shot and killed two U.S. soldiers for cutting down a poplar tree that was growing on the border and impeding the view of United Nations observers.

Today, he explained, the soldiers simply glare at each other across the border.

As the lecture ended, the group began to reboard the bus. Ainsley looked over. Kyung-joon was standing at the rear of the group, arms crossed as usual, watching her.

"I'm going to ask Kyung-joon about lunch," she said.

"Good luck," whispered Hanna.

Ainsley approached the hawkish escort. "Kyung-joo, what do we eat for lunch?"

The man's mouth tightened. "No lun-che today. You eat dinner only."

"But we're hungry. I have to run the half-marathon tomorrow."

He shook his head. "Dinner is at hotel."

"That's not fair."

"No lun-che." Then Kyung-joo caught her gaze. "Tomorrow you run full mara-ton."

His eyes were dark splinters of ice. Ainsley felt them boring into her skull. She couldn't sense if he'd discovered the bribe or not. She could sense, however, that this wasn't the time or place to argue anything.

"Okay," she replied.

Ainsley felt a scowl cross her face as she turned to reboard the bus. She couldn't finish this assignment quickly enough.

CHAPTER NINETEEN

Five hours later, with the sun dipping below the Pyongyang skyline, the bus rolled up to the Yanggakdo International Hotel.

Inside, Ainsley had curled up in her seat. She'd long ago descended into the miserable depths of low blood sugar. Hunger pains doubled up her belly. Even Hanna had stopped trying to make conversation with her.

At the DMZ, Ainsley had endured three hours of traipsing around concrete bunker-like buildings. Then she'd suffered through a half-hour-long description of the blue U.N. buildings that stand directly athwart the border. She'd stood, bored, in the famous plain room with a microphone and table where the armistice agreement had been signed. She'd gazed at the Bridge of No Return, that symbol of Korean freedom, and been able to think about only one thing.

Fried chicken.

Nearly twenty-four hours without food, and Ainsley couldn't think of anything else. It didn't matter how concerned she was supposed to be with the ideological conflict playing out in slow-motion. She just wanted to push food into her mouth.

"Ainsley," said Hanna.

"What?"

"Does that seem normal to you?"

Her roommate was pointing out the window. Standing on the curb, in front of the hotel, were four soldiers, all standing stiffly. Their eyes were fixated on the bus as it pulled up.

"Nothing seems normal here," answered Ainsley.

The brakes chunked hard, the bus stopped, and the door hissed open. Kyung-hee sprang to his feet. "Remember, dinner is served in thirty minutes in Conference Room A."

Ainsley filed out down the steps. The soldiers in olive drab soldiers waited, two on each side, peering up the stairs into the interior. Their hands gripped the strap of their weapons, slung over their backs.

They were waiting for somebody.

As Ainsley walked past them, she felt her throat go dry. They ignored her.

Entering the hotel lobby, Ainsley crouched next to a pillar, pretending to tie her shoe. In reality, she was watching the soldiers.

As the last of the tourists stepped off the bus, Kyung-hee came down the stairs, his head bowed. Kyung-joon was behind him, dark frown on his face, pushing at his partner's back with strange stabby little chops. Kyung-hee paused on the last step, closed his eyes, and threw his head back. A long stream of anguished syllables streamed out of his mouth. The soldiers waited impassively.

When he stepped onto the cement, the four soldiers grabbed him, two at each arm. They escorted him to a waiting military vehicle, pushed him into the back seat, and closed the doors. The vehicle roared off.

Ainsley remained crouched, her fingers frozen on her laces.

The escort was gone. Kyung-hee had just been detained by his own government.

Removed from his duty.

Who knows where he could be taken? Possibly sent off to the political camps. That wasn't just her imagination, either. The labor camps, mostly in the northern half of the country, held hundreds of thousands of political prisoners. They're clearly visible in satellite photos. There, people were hung by their skin from hooks over firepits. Others were forced to stand in crane pose for hours until their knees broke down. The diet consisted of gruel, rats, insects, and sometimes feces. Children killed parents for a bowl of corn. Doctors performed surgery without anesthesia.

They were the worst places on earth.

Kyung-hee was headed there—and it was her fault. Ainsley was sure of it. Had someone seen them speaking near the bathroom in the restaurant? Or had they caught him when he attempted to change Ainsley's registration?

She let her imagination roam. He had a family. What would happen to them? They might be rounded up too.

All because she didn't want to run two extra hours.

Ainsley could feel her brain starting to short-circuit. All this was too much to battle. The regime was like a wall of rammed earth. It showed no mercy.

She stood up, felt her head start to swim, then leaned into the pillar to steady herself. She couldn't tell if it was shock or hunger.

Hanna appeared at her side. Her face was calm but her voice betrayed urgency. "Did you see that?"

"Yeah."

"I truly hope your bribe didn't have anything to do with that."

Ainsley paused. "This country is just..." She let the sentence die off.

Hanna clasped her hand. "I didn't want to admit this, but I think it's good that we're leaving after the marathon."

The marathon. Ainsley had momentarily forgotten it was tomorrow morning. At this moment, she couldn't imagine running anywhere except to the airport.

"I'm going upstairs to lay down," she said.

The Dutchwoman caught her arm. "But they're serving dinner. Beef with rice. Aren't you starving?"

Ainsley shook her head. "I've just lost my appetite."

CHAPTER TWENTY

Nine o'clock a.m.

Race day.

Outside the Kim Il Sung stadium, Ainsley was waiting in a line of fifty people to use the port-a-potty.

She'd drunk two liters of water before bed, which had led to an interrupted night's sleep. Then she'd drunk another liter of water an hour ago. At breakfast she'd finally managed to shovel a bowl of white rice down her gullet. She was still fighting a massive calorie deficit, no doubt, but at least this mini-carb load would begin to remedy that.

She wore the two layered tops, a blue short sleeve and a black long sleeve, both made of a thin wicking material. In the center of her torso, taped to her shirt, was her number. Below the waist, the charcoal gray pair of running pants. On her feet were her pink-and-white trainers. Nothing new on race day was the rule, of course, but she'd broken that rule with a new pair of run socks. They had blister resistance.

In her mind's eye hung a face.

Kenneth Park.

She'd looked at his photo for a quarter of an hour last

night. It would be an easy face to identify. With that strong jaw, he'd seemed very determined—more like a warrior than a pastor.

Ainsley looked at the thousands of runners around her, mostly Asian but also Caucasian and African. Most of them wore runners' garb in various garish hues. A few were wearing garbage bags over their torsos. That was a cheap but efficient way of keeping heat in the trunk on a cold morning.

As the line inched forward, Ainsley bounced on her toes, cricked her neck, adjusted her sports bra. Then she reviewed the course map in her mind. It was a 10K flat run that looped through the Arch of Triumph, alongside the Friendship Tower, through various tunnels, across bridges.

She would run it four times.

Because that's what she was registered for. A full marathon. And it could not be changed.

Kenneth Park was going to be waiting somewhere alongside the river. That's all she knew. And since she was doing the loop four times, she'd have four attempts to identify him, high-five him, and accept the handoff from him—all without breaking stride.

She had to admit that there was one advantage to running the full marathon. She'd have four chances to make the handoff, instead of only two.

There was a loud blast of fanfare from distant loudspeakers, and a masculine voice spoke urgently in Korean. She couldn't understand the words. She didn't need to. The port-a-potty line fell apart as the runners began to move towards the starting line.

Ainsley followed the crowd. She'd find a toilet somewhere along the racecourse.

Close to the starting line, the runners were squished literally shoulder-to-shoulder. Virtually all were shorter than herself. She looked down at the woman next to her. It was a tiny, nearly dwarf-like creature, wearing a gray cotton t-shirt, blue jeans, a pair of white trainers. Ainsley shook her head. This woman wouldn't even make it one lap, not dressed like that. Nobody could run in denim.

The sound of an orchestra broke out of the speakers, built up into a crescendo—

—and then a loud gunshot sounded.

Around her, the runners broke out jogging. Ainsley started running too, swept along by the power of the crowd.

Within minutes the course had carried her beneath a massive square arch, constructed of white marble. Without breaking stride, Ainsley craned her head to marvel at it. This was the Arch of Triumph. She recognized it from her reading. It'd been modeled on the one in Paris, but ten meters taller. It commemorated Korea's victory over the Japanese in 1945.

Twenty minutes in, and the runners had already begun to separate. The better ones, the professionals, were already far ahead, out of sight. The worse ones, already out of breath, were lagging far behind. Ainsley concentrated on keeping her comfortable medium pace—not too fast, not too slow.

Before long, Ainsley found herself running through a long tunnel lit orange by artificial lights. The construction was immaculate, as though the concrete had been poured yesterday. She concentrated on her legwork and focused her eyes on the small circle of natural light at the far end.

When she emerged into the daylight, the course took a swift dogleg, and she suddenly found herself running along a river to her left. Access was blocked by a thick balustrade. To her right, a line of onlookers crowded the sidewalk, standing four and five deep behind thick metal stanchions.

She suddenly sucked in her breath.

This was where Kenneth Park was to be stationed. Along the river.

Ainsley moved to the right side of the street, close to the

people, and slowed her pace. She watched the onlookers' faces slide past her. Maybe they laughed and cried and sympathized with family at home, but in public these people were emotional slabs of stone. Their eyes watched her with a blank gaze.

One block, two blocks, three blocks. The array of local Pyongyang faces seemed to never end.

But no Kenneth Park.

The course bent away and crossed the river, and soon Kim Il Sung stadium came into sight again.

The first 10K. Three more laps to find him.

Tightening her hands into fists, Ainsley steeled herself to keep running.

CHAPTER TWENTY-ONE

Forty-five minutes later, Ainsley plunged into the orange-lit concrete tunnel for the second time. Her breathing was more labored now. Her pace had slowed. Her arms stayed a little closer to her sides.

She emerged from the tunnel and swung around the dogleg and found the river to her left once again. On her right was the gauntlet of spectators. As before, she slowed down and scanned the faces.

This time, she saw him.

Kenneth Park.

His face was unmistakable. The solid chin, the determined eyes. Kenneth was also a full head higher than the other spectators. It was a clear sign of a Western diet. Ainsley wondered how he could hide in plain sight in this country, despite his own genetic heritage.

They locked eyes. Something was different about Kenneth's gaze. It somehow seemed more Western.

Ainsley lifted her index finger and swirled it around. Next lap.

Kenneth saw the gesture. He nodded.

The third lap.

And then Ainsley passed him. Moving on towards the Arch of Triumph, and the halfway point, she felt rejuvenated. The transfer of the onyx teacup was going to happen, and as long as she didn't drop the damn thing, she would bring it back to her hotel room, privately victorious.

But first she had to run the third lap.

———

An hour later, her pace had slowed significantly.

Approaching the three-quarters mark, Ainsley realized that she had never run this far in her life, ever. Her body was beginning to show the effects. She could feel something, a tendon maybe, tightening up the side of her right leg. Despite the new socks, blisters were forming on the backs of her heels. Most annoyingly, both ball-and-socket joints of her pelvis were beginning to ache.

Ainsley knew what was happening. She was hitting the wall.

It's a phenomenon well known to runners. It happens when glycogen stores are depleted, and a body literally has no more fuel to propel itself.

She could tell that she'd lost mental energy too. Her concentration, normally so strong, had evaporated. Her mind was stumbling all over like a punch-drunk boxer—pieces of phrases, snatches of musical lyrics, bits of blurred memories.

Then Ainsley plunged into the orange-lit tunnel for the third time. The lights seemed somehow softer. She started to imagine that they were orange wall sconces in a softly-lit European restaurant. She could almost smell the wine and cheese and soup and bread and olives.

Ainsley swung around the sharp dogleg for the third time and forced herself to concentrate. She flexed her fingers, preparing for the handoff. She would do it fast. It would be unnoticeable to anybody who wasn't looking.

Then Ainsley saw a strange figure ahead. It was a small woman in a gray cotton t-shirt, stylish blue jeans, and a pair of white trainers. Her legs were moving with impossibly tiny strides, literally no more than a few centimeters at a time, and she was hugging the right side of the street, close enough to touch the spectators.

It was the dwarfish creature from the starting line.

Ainsley smiled. She'd just lapped the poor woman, completed nearly three 10Ks in the time it had taken the woman to run two. That was no surprise. The surprise was the fact that the woman had made it as far as she had while wearing a pair of denim jeans.

Then she saw him.

Kenneth Park.

His head rose above the other onlookers. He was about twenty meters ahead and had moved to the railing. Ainsley flexed her hand in preparation for the handoff.

She came up behind the dwarfish woman in the jeans. The creature was moving slower than a snail in a wheelchair. Ainsley made a quick decision. If she raced around the woman, it would draw attention to herself, and she risked missing Kenneth Park. He was less than ten meters away.

It was wiser to slow down and stay behind the woman.

Then the dwarfish creature threw up her hands, uttered a strange warbled cry—

—and fell down. Flat on the concrete.

After nearly three hours of running, Ainsley was slow to react. She was upon the woman before she knew it. She tried to leap over her body, but the toe of her trainer hooked in the hem of the woman's jeans.

Ainsley felt her arms windmilling through the air. Then

she felt her knees hit concrete, followed by her elbows, then her chest, and finally her face.

She'd tripped over the dwarfish woman in the jeans.

A weird cry rose up from the onlookers. Ainsley turned her head. A mass of North Korean spectators had clumped around the restraining barrier, jostling each other for a better view of the fallen Westerner.

She lifted her head and scanned the crowd. Kenneth Park was gone.

Shit.

Her cheek on the concrete, Ainsley closed her eyes and cursed quietly. Too much attention: Kenneth Park had bolted. All eyes were on her. There was no way to make the exchange on this lap.

She wearily tried to hoist herself up to her knees. Then she felt hands on her arms and back. It was a pair of medics. They forced her to sit down on the concrete.

Ainsley sipped from a cup of water while they dressed her scraped knees, elbows, and cheek. She watched the other runners pounding past her. A wall of cell phones recorded her. She was possibly the most interesting thing they'd ever seen.

At last the medics helped her to her feet. Ainsley slowly began to walk, then broke into a slow, limping jog. Her mind seized upon a single thought.

She only had one more chance to get the onyx teacup.

CHAPTER TWENTY-TWO

Three hours and forty-five minutes after the start of the marathon, Ainsley plunged into the orange tunnel for the fourth and last time.

She was barely jogging at this point. The blisters on her heels felt like gaping wounds, irritating her more with every step. Her legs were long tubes of liquefied butter. The inside of her thighs had begun to chafe severely, despite the promise of anti-chafe pants. She would've traded a week's salary for a finger of petroleum jelly.

The ointment on her scraped cheek had dribbled down the side of her face into the corner of her mouth. It tasted like bitter herbs.

Worst of all, there was a van following about twenty meters behind her.

Ainsley knew why. She'd fallen to the very back of the pack. The organizers of the Mangyongdae Marathon had made it abundantly clear that runners were given four hours to complete the marathon—no more, no less. There was no room for stragglers. She only had fifteen minutes to get back to the stadium.

But she didn't care about finishing the race.

She exited the tunnel and swung around the dogleg for the fourth and final time. Once again, the course opened up, the river to her left, the spectators to her right. The crowd had already thinned out. Many had probably already walked to the stadium for the closing ceremonies.

Her eyes scanned the remaining heads along the barrier. No sign of Kenneth. She hoped that he hadn't been spooked by the previous lap.

With only one more block before the street swung away from the river, Ainsley slowed herself to a walk. She gazed at the faces that watched her curiously. It couldn't end like this. She'd travelled too far. Pastor Jeong and his immigrant church had too much on the line.

A swift movement caught her eye. A man had appeared along the barrier at the very end of the block. He stood a head taller than the others.

Kenneth Park.

They locked eyes. Ainsley nodded. He nodded back.

Kenneth leaned over the barrier, as though pretending to get a better view of the runners.

Six steps—

Five steps—

Kenneth held his hand up, his fingers closed upon something.

Four—

Gasping with exertion, Ainsley willed herself to go on.

Three—

She wiped her right palm on her shorts.

Two—

She lifted her right hand and opened her palm.

One—

They locked eyes—

Their hands met—

Kenneth's hand felt cold and soft. In his hand was a hard object. Ainsley closed her palm upon it.

Another stride, and their hands fell apart. She was a step past him, then two steps past, then three.

She felt the item safe in her palm.

Ainsley's eyes grew suddenly bright. Her lungs filled with air. Her heart bloomed in her chest. Energy filled her body.

She'd done it. She'd made the exchange. Then she looked down at the object in her hand, and her heart sank.

It wasn't an onyx teacup.

It was a thin canister.

CHAPTER TWENTY-THREE

Ainsley's face fell. The tiny plastic container had a cap on one end. It was about the thickness of a pencil and barely as long as her thumb.

Her eyes flamed with anger. The church hadn't contracted her to find a freaking tube of lipstick. What the hell had he given to her?

Behind her, an engine gunned. Ainsley glanced backwards over her shoulder. It was the van that had been slowly following her.

It was speeding up.

Shit.

The driver had seen the exchange.

Ainsley didn't have any more time to worry about the contents of the canister. She had to worry about keeping it. She quickly stuffed it into her bra, praying that her meager endowment would keep it safe.

Straight ahead was a sign with lettering in Korean. Underneath were the words *Rest station*. She scanned the area. Card tables with tiny cups of water. Garbage cans overflowing with crumpled cups. Staffers sweeping the ground with a wide broom.

Then she saw the port-a-potty.

Perfect. She would open the canister there. In private.

Ainsley angled off the racecourse and walked to the toilet. There was no line. As she reached for the handle—

—a man's hand grabbed her forearm and yanked it back. Startled, Ainsley looked at him. It was a member of the race staff. He wore an intimidating scowl on his face.

"No," he said.

"I go here," she replied, tapping on the bathroom door.

"No," he said, then gestured back to the racecourse. She looked back and saw the van stopped, waiting. Another man stood by the door, hand on the handle.

"There?" she said.

His words came at her like a spray of bullets. "You go there. Ameri-can."

She noted the extra spite dripping from that last syllable. "Into the van?"

"You go there."

His hands pushed at her as if kneading a blob of dough, until she found herself stumbling towards the van. Was she being arrested? Detained? Deported?

She dropped her hands to her sides, a sign of nonresistance. At the van, the man slid open the door. Inside were seven other runners, looking utterly spent. Ainsley quickly sussed out the situation. These were the slowpokes. She was being rounded up to be taken to the stadium for the closing ceremonies. Apparently the slowest runners weren't allowed to finish at their own pace.

She turned to the staffer. "But the stadium is right there. I can finish in ten minutes."

The race staffer's hands chopped and pushed at her back, shoving Ainsley into the van. "You go there."

Reluctantly, she climbed inside with the other runners. Then the door slid shut and the van began to move. Ainsley felt the canister growing warmer against her heart.

They arrived at the gate of the stadium, and Ainsley slowly disgorged from the vehicle. She began to limp towards the stadium entrance. Two minutes of sitting, and her legs had already begun to cramp.

She passed through the opening and emerged onto the broad track that circled the floor of the stadium. Strange orchestral music floated out of unseen speakers. To her left was the finish line, but she needed to run one more lap to arrive at it.

In the middle of the field, behind a rail, were the other runners, nearly two thousand. Some were standing and chatting, sipping from cups. Others had flopped backwards onto the floor of the stadium. A few were being tended to by paramedics.

Towering all around her, in the stadium seats sat one hundred and fifty thousand spectators. As she summoned all her strength to begin running the final lap, she felt the hair on her neck stood on end. The eyes of the entire stadium were upon her at that moment.

The small canister sizzled against her ribcage like a burning secret.

A minute and a half later, she crossed the finish line, barely noticing. Then she was allowed into the field proper, with the other runners. Someone handed her a towel. Another person handed her a large cup of water.

Ainsley moved through the crowd as though in a dream. They were milling about, laying on the ground, doing jumping jacks, laughing, crying. The scent of body odor was strong, even in the cool air. A few were even asleep on the ground.

Ainsley ignored all of them. All she wanted was twenty seconds of privacy to open the canister.

She found a row of portable toilets. The line was stacked twenty deep.

Forget it.

Ainsley finally sat down on the ground and draped the towel over her head. It was dark in here. Nothing but the sensation of her own breath, the chatter of the people around her, the distant lilting violins from the loudspeakers.

Nobody could see her.

She reached into her bra and pulled out the canister. Careful to keep it concealed under the towel, she popped open the cap and tilted the canister upside down.

Nothing came out.

She reached her pinky finger inside and slowly drew it out.

A slip of paper.

A roar went up from the crowd. The sound of exploding fireworks outside the stadium.

Ignoring the commotion outside, Ainsley unrolled the small slip of paper with trembling fingers. On it was a scrawled message.

It was too dark to read beneath the towel, so she pulled it off her head. She saw a riot of red-and-white fireworks exploding in a ring around the stadium. At the gate, a large military procession had entered and begun to march around the track.

Ignoring the ruckus, Ainsley looked down at the note in her hands. She read the words.

She couldn't believe what it said, so she read them a second, then a third, time.

Run to the market. They're coming for you.

CHAPTER TWENTY-FOUR

Ainsley stared at the message, waiting for it to sink into her head.

They're coming for you.

Ainsley's mind raced. The word they could refer to anybody. In this case, though, she was pretty sure who they meant.

The regime.

She felt a zipper of panic run down her spine. In the blink of an eye, Ainsley felt more exposed than she'd ever been. The coating of civil rights that is painted onto middle-class life in Western democracies, the protections that she'd always taken for granted, assumed to be as natural as grass and sun and rain—

—they truly were gone.

Maybe the regime had learned about the onyx scheme. After all, Kenneth Park had been running loose and free and illegal inside the country for quite a while. Or maybe they'd already caught him, and he was being used as a honeypot to ensnare her. Or maybe Kyung-hee had rolled over on her under questioning, and they wanted her for the bribe. Or maybe there was no reason at all. There didn't have to be, not here. North Korea was a place where you could be sentenced to life in a political prison camp for a miniscule crime your grandfather had committed fifty years ago.

Whatever the reason, she could only do one thing. It was the same thing she'd just spent four hours doing.

Run.

Ainsley stood up on aching legs and looked at the military parade. It had completely encircled the field, the olive-uniformed soldiers marching in lockstep. Unlike many of the other runners, she had no interest in marveling at their fascist efficiency. She only wanted to find way to escape.

There were none. They'd closed the stadium exit. She, and the other runners, were locked in here, totally at the mercy of the regime. This could be the final resting site of everybody here, if the regime desired it.

She felt someone touch her elbow. She whirled, arms up in protection.

No need for that. It was Hanna.

"You scared me," Ainsley said.

"It's just me," said the Dutchwoman. "Congratulations on finishing."

"I didn't. They picked me up in the van with ten minutes to go."

Hanna lifted her chin into the air. "Too bad. I was eighteen minutes off my best time. A terrible showing. Honestly, I don't know who can run in these conditions." She lifted her water bottle to her mouth and swallowed. "So you found the guy?"

"Yeah."

Hanna's eyes flashed with excitement. "You have the teacup?"

"No. He gave me this instead."

She handed Hanna the message, and the Dutchwoman read it. "Is this for real?"

"I think so."

Hanna grew a little pale. She handed it back. "But you haven't done anything wrong."

"I bribed an official."

"That's true."

The two women stood on the field of the stadium, safely anonymous in the crowd of runners. Ainsley found herself hunching over, unconsciously trying to stay low.

"So what are you going to do?" asked Hanna.

Ainsley's jaw worked itself left and right. Her eyes were alive with passion. "First, shower and change at the hotel. Then I go to the market."

"Which one?"

"Probably the one we saw in your telescope."

Hanna shook her head. "They'll never let you off the island."

"I'm not going to let myself be taken a political prisoner."

Hanna handed the message back to her. "How do you know can you trust the guy who gave you this?"

"Because he's trying to save his church," said Ainsley, "and because he's a Westerner."

"That makes sense."

"And because I would trust anybody, even my ex-husband, before I trusted this regime."

"That makes two of us," said Hanna. "Let me help you."

"Why?" said Ainsley.

"Because it's exciting." She paused. "And it will make for a great segment on my program."

"I don't know why I like you, Hanna."

The woman smiled. "I've heard that before. Let's go."

CHAPTER TWENTY-FIVE

An hour later, as the bus pulled up to the curb of the Yanggakdo Hotel, Ainsley and Hanna peered outside the window.

In the lobby stood a team of soldiers. They were scanning the runners as they filed out of the buses ahead.

"Ainsley—"

"I know."

She felt Hanna's hand snake around her belly and pull off the paper number that had been plastered against her shirt.

"Now it's harder to identify you," said the Dutchwoman. "Here, take this."

She plastered her own number on Ainsley's back. Then she pulled the visor off her head and placed it on Ainsley's head.

"Thanks," said Ainsley. "Now listen. In the elevator, I'm going to get off at the sixth floor. You go up to our room and check it out. If everything's okay, you come back and get me."

"Where will you be?"

"Waiting next to the elevator. Sixth floor."

"Sixth floor. Got it."

Together the two women stepped off the bus and hurried across the luxurious marble lobby, keeping tight inside a pack of other runners. Ainsley knew it was a partly useless precaution. After all, she was a sitting duck in this hotel. If the regime wanted to get her, they would find a way.

The soldiers watched the passing runners closely. Ainsley kept her head down and the visor pulled low over her face.

After passing the gauntlet, they arrived at the elevator. Ainsley pressed the up button. It didn't light. She jabbed at it ferociously.

"I heard there was an electricity outage this afternoon," said a man.

"So what does that mean?" said Ainsley.

"We probably have to take the stairs."

Several groans issued from the other runners. Hanna spun around. "We just finished a marathon. Are you complaining about doing a little more walking?"

More groans, but the group reluctantly moved towards the nearby stairwell. Ainsley followed at the rear of the pack and peered up the hollow inner portion of the stairwell. It was poorly lit, a caged light bulb on every floor, but otherwise seemed like a staircase found in almost any modern building.

Ainsley began wearily trudging up the staircase. Left foot, right foot. She listened to the slow, weary thuds of the other runners' shoes.

Then she heard something that made her stop.

From the staircase above came the heavy clomp of boots. Harsh guttural voices began barking at each other. Between the echoes and the dialect, the words were unintelligible.

She leaned her head over and peered up. In the dim gray light, she caught a flash of olive drab. A bit of red sash.

Agents of the regime.

And they were coming down the stairs.

Towards her.

She had fifteen seconds at most to decide what to do. Maybe they weren't coming for her. Maybe they were coming from somewhere else in the hotel. There were hundreds and hundreds of other foreigners here.

Still, she couldn't risk getting caught.

To her right was the door marked 5. Ainsley yanked the handle, and it mercifully swung open. She quietly stepped inside and clicked the door shut behind her. Then she looked around.

This may have been the fifth floor of the hotel, but there wasn't a carpet or wall sconce to be found. It was a long hallway with jet black linoleum. A dropped ceiling covered most but not all of the ductwork. Doors opened left and right off the hallway. It was empty at the moment.

This looked a lot like central command. This could be where the regime spied on their visitors.

Ainsley heard the voices in the stairwell growing louder. She saw a closed door nearby. She yanked on the handle and pulled. Locked. She tried a second door. That was locked too.

She saw a third door a few steps away. She darted over and yanked on the handle. It swung open. Inside were three brooms, two buckets, and a shelf's worth of cleaning agents. A fuse box was bolted into the wall.

It was a utility closet.

Ainsley stepped inside and slowly swung the door closed, leaving only a sliver of space between the door and the frame. It would do her no good at all to lock herself inside a utility closet. The weird smell of cleaning solutions assaulted her nostrils. She leaned against the back wall and felt the cold, nubbled surface of the concrete through the material of her shirt.

She heard the door to the stairwell burst open. Peering through the vertical crack, Ainsley saw three military men in olive drab burst into the fifth floor. They headed straight towards the utility closet. Ainsley felt her heart skip a beat. Then she noticed that they were carrying something. It was a duffel bag.

Her duffel bag.

She felt herself growing indignant. Nobody had the right to take her luggage out of her room. Then she had to remind herself, once again, that the normal rules didn't apply here.

The soldiers passed by the closet, their footsteps echoing down the hallway. Then another door slammed, and the silence returned.

She was alone.

Ainsley slunk down to the floor of the closet until she was in a crouch. Then she lifted her head, pushed back the hair from her face—

—and her elbow knocked something off a cradle on the wall. The object fell to the floor and began beeping.

She picked it up. It was a phone. This wasn't only a utility closet. It was also a communications closet.

The dial tone beeped insistently from the piece. Then a name ran across Ainsley's mind.

Eugene.

He'd offered to show her around the city. He even had a car. And he would probably do anything she wanted because he desperately wanted to get laid.

He was her ticket out of here.

Ainsley remembered all the digits of his number except the last one. Had he said a seven instead of a zero, or a zero instead of a seven? She guessed the seven. The call went through. A woman answered with something unintelligible. Ainsley quickly hung up. Wrong guess.

She redialed with the zero. Eugene picked up on the first ring, as though he were waiting for someone to call. "*Yaboseyo.*"

"It's Ainsley."

She could hear him almost sit up. "Whoa, hey, what's happening? You finished the marathon?"

"Yep," she lied.

"And the onyx? You got it?"

"Of course," she lied again. "So, Eugene, it's Saturday night and I don't have anyone to show me the city. I can't just sit around either. They told us we're supposed to walk around to avoid serious cramping."

"So you're calling me," he said.

"How soon can you be here?" she said cheerily.

"Like, ten minutes."

"Even with traffic?"

"There's never traffic in Pyongyang."

"Awesome. I'll be waiting out front."

She replaced the phone on the cradle. It wasn't her fault that Eugene didn't know what he was being roped into.

———

A moment later, Ainsley quietly stepped out of the closet. She walked quickly over to the door and reentered the stairwell.

Then she heard a voice above her, "Ainsley."

She looked up. Hanna was peering down at her. Her face was drawn tightly. "Don't move. I'm coming to you."

Hanna was already running down the stairs. Ainsley admired the fact that she still had energy.

A moment later, she arrived and threw her arms around Ainsley and squeezed hard. Then she pulled back, a serious look on her face. "They dragged all our stuff out into the hallway."

"I saw a man carrying my duffel bag."

"Yeah. They overturned all the furniture in the room."

Ainsley's eyes searched the wall for answers. "Shit."

The Dutchwoman looked at Ainsley. "We're in trouble, Ainsley. A lot of trouble."

Her eyes found Hanna. "Do you know if they took my passport?"

"Was it in your small pouch?"

Ainsley nodded.

Hanna looked sympathetic. "Yes, they did."

Oh God. Ainsley's fingers clutched the railing, squeezing the iron. Her eyes were a pair of lasers fixed upon a distant spot behind Hanna. She felt the rage beginning to gather within her.

Then everything went blurry. Ainsley saw two vertical walls of blackness close in on either side of her vision. She felt Hanna's arm snake around her waist.

Then she hit the floor.

CHAPTER TWENTY-SIX

The voice cut through Ainsley's dream state like a chainsaw through cotton candy.

She recognized the voice. It belonged to Hanna.

Ainsley opened her eyes. She was flat on her back on the stairwell. The Dutchwoman was on her knees, leaning over her.

"Were you talking to me?" said Ainsley.

"I was telling you that you have to wake up," replied Hanna. "You can't be weak right now. You have to be strong."

Ainsley sat up. "How long was I out?"

"Only a minute."

When Ainsley tried to stand, Hanna pushed her down again. "Hold on. Wait until your head clears."

Ainsley leaned herself against the wall. "So I guess we can't go back to the room."

The Dutchwoman shook her head. "But I brought you some candies." She dumped a small pile of hard candies into Ainsley's hand. "They'll give you quick energy."

Ainsley put them into her pocket with barely a glance. "I was really hoping for an ice bath."

"It's not going to happen. Let's get you on your feet."

She helped Ainsley to her feet. Ainsley felt her head clearing up. She could see the next step very clearly. "Hanna, Eugene's coming to pick me up. He doesn't know it, but he's going to help me get to that market."

"So you're really going to trust this guy who was supposed to give you the teacup."

"It's my only hope."

Hanna sighed. "Well, I'm coming too."

"No, you're not."

She leveled a serious gaze at Ainsley. "I already told you, I am a television producer. This is a story, and I'm involved whether you like it or not. Plus, I'm good insurance for you."

"Why?"

"If they detain us, there will be an international uproar." Hanna pulled herself up to her full height. "I'm highly visible. I know most of the European news media. We look out for one another."

Ainsley shrugged. "If you insist. Here's what we do. We have to cross the lobby. I'm going to bend over, and you're going to keep my face covered."

"Let's do it."

The women circled down the stairwell and entered the lobby. Ainsley began to affect a horrific limp, though truth be told she didn't have to try that hard. Her face winced in pain, her hand reached down and clutched her knee. Hanna played the role of nurse perfectly, walking alongside Ainsley, arm flung across her shoulders, pretending to nurse her.

The soldiers were facing away from them, scanning the other competitors who were emerging from the buses as they arrived at the hotel curb. Together, they limped past the soldiers, through the revolving doors, and out into the hotel grounds.

They moved down the footpath and through the trees. A

breeze ruffled the treetops. Ainsley couldn't see the river splitting on either side of the island, but she could sense it was there.

"How far are we going?" asked Hanna.

"Just a little more."

Arriving at the head of the path, Ainsley saw a Pyeonghwa Pronto GS idling. It was a new mini SUV. Behind the wheel was Eugene. He waved. Then his face fell as he saw Hanna.

Ainsley quickly climbed into the backseat of the vehicle, Hanna right behind her. They shut the door.

Eugene turned around, his face in utter confusion. "You didn't change? And who's this?"

"I'm Hanna," said the Dutchwoman, "and you need to drive us off this island."

"Ainsley? Is this for real?"

She tried to speak calmly. "Eugene, listen—I'm in real trouble. I need you to take me to the market."

"What kind of trouble?"

"I lied to you. The guy didn't give me the onyx teacup. He gave me this instead."

Ainsley showed Eugene the note. He read it, then looked back at her. "This is too much. I mean, it's dangerous. I shouldn't even be here with you."

"It's too late," said Hanna, "because we're in your vehicle. And it's more dangerous if she stays."

"They already ripped apart our hotel room," added Ainsley.

Ainsley could see that Eugene was regretting having come to pick her up. His dream of having a date with a Westerner had fallen apart.

"There are several markets. Which one do you think he means?"

Ainsley shrugged. "Your guess is as good as mine. Maybe the biggest one? Is there one that everybody knows?"

Eugene nodded. "It's not too far."

"You can get us off the island?"

Eugene nodded and waved a badge at her. "I'm an official guide. Full access until Saturday. But they're going to ask for your names and room number."

"Can we lie?"

Eugene looked thoughtful. "I know the guard who's on duty right now and it might work."

"You're thinking what I'm thinking?" said Hanna.

"We lie?" said Ainsley.

"Outrageously."

"Let's try it."

Ainsley watched as Eugene threw the car into drive and whipped around the small island until he pulled up to the guardhouse at the foot of the bridge. A gate arm blocked them from proceeding.

The guard emerged from the small guardhouse and approached the car. Eugene rolled down his window, showed him his badge, and spoke with him in rapid Korean.

The guard pointed his fingers at the women. "He wants your names and room number," said Eugene.

Hanna leaned forward. "Our names are Julia Roberts and Jodie Foster. Room fourteen-oh-eight."

Eugene turned and repeated it in Korean. Ainsley didn't know how he kept a straight face doing it. The guard went to the registry in his guardhouse and scanned the list of hotel guests.

"Julia Roberts and Jodie Foster," Eugene said again.

The guard looked flustered as his eyes darted around the screen.

"What's happening?" said Ainsley.

"He's a substitute," said Eugene. "All the usual guards who read English were pulled to work the marathon this afternoon. Watch this."

He stepped out of the vehicle and stood alongside the man. He pointed to the name on the screen and explained something.

"Oh my God," said Hanna, "he's teaching the guy bad English."

Ainsley watched the interaction and listened closely. Sure enough, Eugene was showing the guards how the name Julia was spelled S-u-s-a-n.

The guard nodded in agreement. Eugene returned to the car. The gate arm swung up, and he quickly floored the accelerator. The mini SUV flew across the bridge.

"You're terrible," said Hanna.

"You should thank me," said Eugene. "I just smuggled your ass out of the hotel where agents of the state are trying to find you."

"Thank you," said Ainsley.

"You're welcome. And now let's find the *jangmadang* so I can get you out of my car."

CHAPTER TWENTY-SEVEN

The car sped down the boulevard. Four o'clock in the afternoon, and the street was almost totally empty.

Ainsley looked out the window. In the middle of an intersection, a woman in a crisp blue uniform with white bobby socks and black heels stood on a riser inside a circle of chalk. In her right hand was a red-and-white striped baton. She was waiting to direct non-existent traffic.

Ainsley had heard about these traffic girls. Symbols of Pyongyang and therefore the regime, they came from loyal families, and were often the prettiest that the country had to offer. But with few people wealthy enough to purchase automobiles, the girls had become mostly decorative.

"Eugene, do you know where you're going?" said Hanna.

"Yes," he replied.

"Because if it's the market I spotted it in my telescope, it was about two blocks behind us, and three more blocks to the right."

He was looking at her in the rearview mirror. "You brought a telescope?"

"Of course."

"No wonder they tore apart your room."

He slowed the car down and executed a U-turn. Then he went back two blocks and turned left.

Hanna turned to Ainsley. "Once we get there, what are you going to do?"

"I'm going to ask if anybody knows Kenneth Park," she replied.

"Easier said than done."

"You have a better idea?"

Eugene slowed the car again and pulled alongside the curb. Then he put it into park. "This is as far as your taxi goes. The market is straight ahead."

"Thank you again," said Ainsley. She paused. "I'm sorry that I lied to you."

He mustered a weak smile. "I don't know why you're thanking me. We never met."

"He drove Julia Roberts and Jodie Foster," said Hanna.

"One more thing," he said.

Ainsley paused, her fingers on the handle. "What?"

"Don't call me again."

The two women exited the car. He immediately drove off.

Ainsley felt a shiver of fear. They were now two unescorted foreign women in Pyongyang.

Alone... and illegal.

————

The street narrowed as they moved down it.

The buildings on either side were Soviet-era construction, gray and perpendicular and depressing. Ahead, on the left was an alley. It looked oddly familiar. Then Ainsley remembered—this was where she'd spotted the romantic couple in the telescope. She lifted her face upwards. Directly overhead was the lurid billboard of the American GI with a sledgehammer smashing into his skull. This close, it looked even worse. She could almost feel the blood and brain matter falling onto her own head.

Then Ainsley felt even more exposed than she had in the stadium. She no longer had the benefit of a pack of Western runners around her, or an official number on her chest, or the protective cocoon of a sanctioned tour bus. Now she was just a foreigner sticking her big foreign nose where it had been expressly forbidden to go, and without any rights or recourse should things go wrong.

But things wouldn't go wrong. She had to believe that.

The sound of hubbub reached their ears. "It sounds like it's coming from just around that corner," said Hanna.

"Faster," said Ainsley.

They hurried the last two blocks and turned the corner. They found themselves at the edge of the *jangmadang*.

The market.

It was nothing more than a grungy city square, but it was humming with commercial exchange. Currency thrust into hands, goods lifted off tables. It looked better through the telescope.

Ainsley scanned the array of modern items that lay on the low tables. It was surprising. New boxed Panasonic televisions. Stacks of neatly folded khaki pants. Sacks of new basketballs. Cartons of Chinese cigarettes. Chocolate bars. Instant noodles. Chinese electronic tablets. She was most surprised to see cans of Coca-Cola, the evil imperialist beverage.

Pressed against the tables were a mass of shoppers. They stood three deep in places, and these particular ones didn't seem too poor. Several held new mobile phones pressed to their ears. The women wore high heels and stylish skirts. One sported a Coach bag. This was no different from any other capital city where wealthy people manipulated the political system to line their own pockets.

Hanna's eyes grew wider than dinner plates. "We might be the first Westerners to ever see this."

"Doubtful," said Ainsley.

"I would give my salary to have a camera crew right now."

"Where do you think all this stuff comes from?"

"It's probably all smuggled from China." The Dutchwoman paused. "You know, I just noticed something."

"What?"

"Women are running the market."

Ainsley scanned the tables. Sure enough, a middle-aged woman stood behind each pile of goods, without exception.

"I can see it now," said Hanna. "Rising female entrepreneurial class in North Korea. Tonight at eleven." She drove one hand into the other, her eyes flashing. "This would make an incredible segment, wouldn't it?"

Ainsley nodded. "You know what else? I bet these women make a lot more money than their husbands."

"Illegal always pays better," replied Hanna. "That's why people do it."

Ainsley noticed that they'd become the objects of interest. There were quick elbows, furtive glances, side-mouthed whispers. The women at the stalls craned their heads to catch a glimpse of the two Westerners. Ainsley noticed a few people even slipped out of the opposite side of the market. She guessed it could be dangerous to even be seen in a place where you could speak freely to a couple of foreigners.

"Let's walk," said Ainsley.

They moved along the tables. A short woman tended a black cauldron of noodles like a demented witch. A man who looked like a guard over the market came up behind the witch and tapped her forcefully on her shoulder. She grimaced, pulled a fistful of dirty currency from her pocket, twisted around, and stuffed the grimy bills into his open hand.

The Dutchwoman laughed. "So that's how things really work here."

"Bribery."

"And rice theft."

"What do you mean?"

Hanna pointed to several burlap sacks of rice on the ground. On the bags were printed the English words *NFP: National Food Program*.

"That's right," said Hanna, "they're selling relief food."

"I don't believe it," said Ainsley. "That's supposed to be charity for starving people."

Hanna nodded. "One crewman with a handheld camera. That's all I want."

Ainsley felt a shiver of panic. She was beginning to feel that coming to this market had been a mistake. Had Kenneth Park's message been a cheap sadistic trick? He could've run off with the teacup, if it even existed in the first place. This entire assignment should've been scotched from the beginning.

"I've got to talk to someone," she said.

Then Ainsley felt a presence at her elbow. She turned and found herself looking into a furious, hawkish face.

Kyung-joon.

CHAPTER TWENTY-EIGHT

Ainsley attempted to move around the tour escort. She felt him lift a metal baton and press it across her chest, slowly pinning her against the wall. His nostrils were flared, his face a mask.

"Miss Wokker," he said, "you make trouble."

Hanna stepped forward. "Get that baton off her—"

As she reached to touch him, Kyung-joon suddenly made a quick movement with his other hand. It was a cross between a karate chop and a finger flick, and it connected with the Dutchwoman's neck.

Hanna stumbled backwards, clutching her throat as though she'd just been bitten by a snake. "Oh my God, what was that, that hurt—"

Feeling the cold baton pressing hard against her chest, Ainsley willed herself to stay calm.

"You leave hotel without permission," he said.

She didn't reply. Then they were interrupted by a distant noise that quickly grew enormous. *Whoompa whoompa whoompa*. It was the roar of an engine. Its echo was fearsome, and she felt the building reverberate against her spine with its force.

"What is that?" said Hanna.

"I don't know," said Ainsley.

A large military vehicle roared into the opposite side of the market, then stopped. It looked like a low, wide boat and was of a foreign design, possibly Soviet. The long muzzle of a machine gun poked out of a tiny front turret.

It was an armored personnel carrier. A yawning pit opened where Ainsley's stomach used to be.

Terror.

A side hatch popped open, and military officers began to pour out. Some were dressed in ordinary uniforms. All carried their weapons at the ready.

"That thing had better not be here for us," said Ainsley.

"I think it is," said Hanna.

Kyung-joon made a quick whistle, glanced at the carrier, and lifted his arm over his head.

Hanna saw her opportunity. She hauled back and drove her palm into his jaw.

Kyung-joon fell backwards, disoriented, shaking his head. The metal baton fell away from Ainsley's chest.

"Run!" shouted Hanna, grabbing Ainsley's arm.

As the two women bolted, the market erupted into chaos. Shoppers were shrieking, running in every direction at once, trying to push their way out.

The regime had decided to crack down on the private markets.

The two women sprinted around the corner and joined the stream of citizens pouring down the street, back towards the boulevard. Ainsley's eyes were pasted wide open in pure panic.

"Where do we go?" said Hanna.

Ainsley saw the alley again, the one below the anti-U.S.

propaganda, the one where the lovers had been smooching days earlier. "There. Just for the moment."

The women dodged to the right side of the street and plunged into the alley. It was only a few meters wide, lined by a gray concrete warehouse on each side. The walls were unbroken except for a large rolling door on the left.

At the far end of the alley was another pair of teenagers, locked together in an end-of-the-world type of embrace. Some things were universal.

"Do you think we're safe here?"

"As long as they didn't see us run in."

"We could increase our odds."

"How?"

She nodded towards the making-out couple. "We do that."

Ainsley recoiled. "I'm not kissing you."

"No, but we can stand together and hide our faces."

That made sense. They ran to the dead end of the alley. The liplocked young couple looked up, alarmed. "*Gyesog*," said Ainsley. *Continue*.

The lovers went back to each other. She and Hanna faced each other. Ainsley's mouth went dry. She was nervous.

"Don't delay," said Hanna.

"You first."

They drew close to one another in an embrace. Ainsley's hands met in the small of Hanna's back. They pressed their right cheeks together. Their chests were squished together.

"This feels like slow dancing at the worst high school dance ever," said Ainsley.

"You smell disgusting," said Hanna.

"Shut up."

"If this is the last time we meet, I want you to remember that we had a good time."

Ainsley tried to figure out how to respond to that. This

woman truly thought everything with the regime was a big game. Then a distant sound broke the tension.

Whoompa whoompa whoompa.

Oh God.

The women flung themselves together again. Ainsley shut her eyes and hid her face against Hanna's cheek.

The sound grew nearly deafening. Ainsley opened her eyes and peered towards the street. The armored personnel carrier was rolling slowly by the mouth of the alley. *Whoompa whoompa whoompa.*

A moment later, it was gone. The soldiers had passed them. Ainsley felt herself crumple with relief.

"I think we're safe," she said.

Then the armored personnel carrier slowly rolled back into view. It had reversed.

They'd been spotted.

Shit.

"What is it?" said Hanna.

"Don't move."

Ainsley mouthed a silent prayer to a deity that she only at this moment had truly believed in. She felt Hanna's fingers tighten in the flesh of her own back.

The sound of a metallic chunk. Ainsley dared another glance. The hatch had opened. The soldiers were pouring out like heavily armed clowns from a circus car.

And they were running down the alley. Towards them.

Kyung-joon was the last one out.

Loud shouts from the men up front. Next to Ainsley, the adolescent star-crossed lovers broke apart and sprinted past the soldiers, towards the street. The soldiers let the teenagers pass, smacking them on the heads as they fled.

Ainsley and Hanna found themselves alone at the end of the alley. They were cornered.

"This is it," said Hanna.

"We're doomed," said Ainsley.

They reluctantly disengaged from their embrace. Ainsley was numb with exhaustion and fear. The world had slowed to quarter speed. The mere act of turning around felt like pushing through cold porridge.

Nonetheless, she turned wearily towards the men, her hands hanging limply at her side.

Three of the soldiers were kneeling, their weapons trained upon her. She saw three others standing behind them, handcuffs at the ready. Nearby was Kyung-joon, a portrait of impassivity.

"You leave hotel," he spat.

"I had to stretch my legs," she replied.

Nobody batted an eye. The weapons stayed trained on her.

"Look, it's my fault," she said. "Do what you want with me, but let Hanna go."

Kyung-joon said something to the men with the handcuffs. They started to step forward when a loud horn sounded. Every member of the military squad whirled.

Behind them, at the mouth of the alley, a van had rolled up next to the armored personnel carrier. Its side door had rolled open.

Leaping out of the vehicle was a team of what appeared to be four commandos.

CHAPTER TWENTY-NINE

Ainsley had never seen a group like this. Four men of different ages and heights, but all dressed in black paramilitary garb—black combat shirts with camouflaged arms, black pants rolled into black boots. They wore no insignias on their clothing. From the way they had held themselves, she sensed that they hadn't had much formal training.

She wondered who this ragtag group was.

One of them stepped forward. He was short, like many North Korean men, but brimming with confidence. Strutted hard. Ainsley sensed that he was one ten-gallon hat short of being a cowboy.

Pointing at the two women, the paramilitary cowboy barked a few words at Kyung-joon, who waved him off. He wasn't easily put off. He barked the same phrase again, then added a few more words with extra emphasis, stabbing his finger at Kyung-joon.

"What's happening?" whispered Hanna.

"I don't know."

Ainsley watched the paramilitary cowboy take a few steps forward and bark something else. Kyung-joon sighed, then pointed at his men's weapons. The muzzles dropped to the cement. The two men stepped forward and met, standing a safe distance apart. It was a parley. The cowboy spoke rapidly, gesturing at Ainsley.

Then he held out a wad of paper.

Bills.

A sneer spread across Kyung-joon's face as he looked at the offer.

"Ani," he said. No.

The paramilitary cowboy didn't blanch. He reached into his pants pocket and thrust out another wad of cash.

As she watched the exchange, Ainsley felt her legs trembling. There wasn't much more juice left in them. She had the sense that she had become chattel, a cow for purchase, but she hadn't the faintest idea which side she should hope to be captured by. The most likely possibility was that one was bad, and the other was worse.

Her hand curled into Hanna's, and the two women held tightly to one another.

Kyung-joon looked at the second bribe. His nose scrunched up. Then he reached forward, took the money, and jerked his thumb over his shoulder.

Towards the women.

The paramilitary cowboy gestured to his men. Ainsley saw Kyung-joon hand several bills to each member of his squad.

Ainsley tensed as Kyung-joon's goons stepped aside and the four paramilitary men stepped forward. She instinctively planted her left foot slightly ahead and lifted her fists. Hanna did the same.

"Do we kick or bite?" said Ainsley.

"Both," said Hanna.

The black-clad squad surrounded Ainsley. Four of them, one at each corner. She spun around, looking for a way out. There was no way out.

So she tried to bolt.

The men caught her on the second step. Ainsley shrieked, writhed, twisted—but their hands were firmly on her. She fell to the ground. Kicked out, screamed. Through the hair in her face, Ainsley saw that Hanna had leapt onto the back of one of the men.

Then she saw Kyung-joon's men pull the Dutchwoman off and haul her away. Her screams reached Ainsley's ears.

She felt a rag suddenly clamped over her nose. A hand held it there with unbelievable pressure. She tried rip it away but the men had pinned down her hands. She shrieked, then nearly gagged when she inhaled.

The rag held a sweet, antiseptic smell. Almost gluey, with the faintest scent of almonds.

Ainsley made a tremendous effort to stand up, but the men had her down. She was hyperventilating, her lungs wracking themselves in huge bursts.

The first thing to go was her clarity of thought. Everything went a bit woozy. Next her muscles relaxed. One more inhale, and Ainsley noticed that her hearing went sideways. The grunts and barked orders sounded as though they were coming from the far end of a tunnel.

Another inhale, and her heartbeat slowed. Her blood pressure was lowering.

Slowly, the shapes of the men's heads lost their definition. Now they were just blurry forms. Her vision irised to a tiny circle—

—and then everything went dark.

CHAPTER THIRTY

Scritch.

Scritch scritch.

The distant sound was like a bird on a tree branch, tweeting happily about its freedom. Ainsley tried to ignore it.

Scritch scritch scritch scritch.

She blinked open her eyes.

Blackness. But not total—there was vague, suffused light. She felt fabric tickling the flesh of her face. She felt her own breath warming her nose and cheeks.

Then she figured it out. There was a bag on her head.

Her mouth dry, Ainsley tried to wet her lips. There was no saliva, so she stopped. Then she tried to orient herself in space. She could feel that she was laying on her side, her knees pulled up towards her chest.

The cushion suddenly heaved up and down. Ainsley felt her body go airborne for a second, then crash down.

She was in a vehicle. In the back seat.

Groggy, she tried to bring her hands around to the front of her body to push herself up, but they wouldn't budge. They were stuck behind her back.

Then it dawned on her. She was handcuffed.

"Help," she said.

It came out like a whisper. She tried it again. This time, a croak.

She heard Korean voices began to speak.

Then it all came rushing back. The flight from the market. The alley. Kyung-joon. The paramilitary squad. The struggle.

She was in the paramilitary squad's vehicle.

Panicking, she tried to yell. It came out sounding more like a weird gargle.

A voice barked an order. Ainsley felt rough hands at her neck. They yanked the fabric off her head. Light flooded her vision, blinding her. She squinched up her eyes and buried her face in the cushion.

She felt the hands fussing with her wrists, and suddenly she was cut free from the cuffs. Her left arm flopped over her body and down to the floor of the vehicle. She didn't feel it hit.

The men's hands gripped her shoulders and forced her to a sitting position. Ainsley had no control over her body. Her head lolled to the left. Her legs pointed to the right. She was a ragdoll.

But at least she was alive.

For now.

Her eyes took in the interior of the vehicle. She was on the middle bench. Two members of the squad occupied the front seats. The paramilitary cowboy in the passenger seat, jaw thrust out, drumming his fingers on the window ledge. Behind her, on the rear bench, were the other two.

The van was bumping down a rutted single-lane road. She looked outside the window. It seemed like a scene from the seventeenth century. Empty brown fields, the earth divided into long runnels for the spring planting. Here and there a row of bare brown poles stood like sentinels in the earth, waiting for someone to string wires across them. Otherwise, this was empty land under empty sky. Not a human settlement anywhere in sight.

This was rural North Korea.

Ainsley felt the panic in her belly again. This squad had driven her out of Pyongyang. Travel outside of the capital wasn't supposed to be possible. Eugene had said so.

Clearly this paramilitary squad had some tricks up its sleeve.

They drove on in silence for another twenty minutes, and the brown fields gave way to small rolling hills. A long white fence appeared on the left side of the road, and the van slowed down. It turned left and went through a gate.

Ainsley cleared her throat. "*Eo di ro ga go it seop ni ga?*" In English: *Where are we going?*

No response.

That was expected. Ainsley wiggled her fingers, then lifted one arm. It still felt like pudding. She couldn't tell if it'd been from the stuff they'd used to knock her out or from having run a full marathon. Most likely both.

The van wound its way through a gently curving road, shaded on both sides by rows of poplars, their branches sprouting with green buds. Then she saw it.

A small country house, nestled into the foothills.

Ainsley cleared her throat. "*Yeo gi eh nu ga sal go it seoup ni ga?*" In English: *Who lives here?*

Still no response. It was possible that they couldn't understand her pronunciation, but more likely they were ignoring her question.

The van slowed to a stop alongside the house. The paramilitary cowboy stepped out of the passenger seat and slid open the side door. He extended his hand to Ainsley.

"Come," he said.

Ainsley paused. He seemed trustworthy enough, but appearances were always deceiving. She thought about bounding past him and making a break for it across the open field, then discarded the idea. Who was she kidding? Better to go along, rebuild her strength, and then escape later.

Reluctantly, she took his offered hand and exited the van.

As her feet hit the ground, her legs immediately buckled. His arm caught her around the waist and held her up.

"Sorry," she said, wincing with the pain.

"Is okay," he replied. "Mara-tan ver-ry ha'd."

True, she thought, the marathon had been very hard. The other members of the squad stepped out of the van. Ainsley felt them surround her.

Then they began to move her towards the front door.

Walking had never felt so torturous. Her legs were melting popsicles, less than a few steps away from dissolving into nothing. Ainsley willed herself forward, feeling the paramilitary cowboy at her side.

She studied the structure. It was low, square, and painted yellow with a red roof. Its walls were punctured with square windows. All told, it looked much like a child's crayon drawing of someone's house.

This clearly wasn't a political camp, she knew that much, but she wasn't going to kid herself. This house was her prison cell. She thought about the rags she would be forced to wear. The hours she would labor in the fields, the burlap bag strapped to her back. The foraging she would be forced to do, if she wanted to eat. She prepared herself for the worst.

The group arrived at the front door. It was a simple unpainted board fitted awkwardly into the frame. There was no stoop. That would be a luxury.

The paramilitary cowboy stepped up and rapped loudly

on the door. Ainsley noticed that his knuckles were gnarled, like a manual laborer's.

They waited. No response.

He rapped again. Shouted something in Korean.

No response.

Ainsley's intestines made a loop-de-loop. Her lips tightened, her nostrils flared.

The cowboy gestured with his hand to follow. Ainsley obediently trailed him around the tiny concrete house towards the back, where a tall wooden fence stood. Into the fence was built a primitive gate, its strap hinges made of cured leather and wire.

The paramilitary cowboy hollered something. A voice on the other side of the fence hollered back.

The man's hand jimmied the latch until it popped open. Then he pushed the gate open and they stepped through the portal.

Ainsley found herself in a large back yard vegetable garden. Eggplants, cucumbers, chestnuts were growing in neat rows. An array of green beans was drying on a rack. There were peppers growing on a wooden trellis clamped onto the slate roof.

And in the middle of the garden, squatting in the dirt, was an old man.

His left hand was held over his eyes, shading them from the late afternoon sun. Broad and hefty, he carried more weight on his frame than most other North Koreans. Tufts of white hair sprouted crazily out of his scalp like stalks of wheat. His skin was pale white and his nose and cheeks were reddened.

The man's gaze landed on her, and he removed his hand to get a better look. When Ainsley saw his face, she nearly gasped.

His eyes were blue.

This was a white man.

He stood up. A smile crept onto his face like a secret being revealed.

"Miss Walker," he said, "I was worried that we weren't going to find you."

CHAPTER THIRTY-ONE

Ainsley's mouth worked itself open and shut. She was a fish yanked out of the ocean and flopping at the bottom of a boat.

The old white man hobbled over, leaning heavily upon the knob of a wooden cane.

He offered her his hand and spoke in his American voice. "I'm William Yaris. A pleasure to finally meet you."

Finally? She took his hand and shook it. "Ainsley Walker."

He looked down at their handshake, seemingly lost in recollection. "It's been a long time since I greeted somebody like this."

Ainsley stood there, immobile, trying to take it all in.

"I just ran a marathon," she said. "And then I went to the market because somebody told me to. That's where these men kidnapped me."

The old man remained stoic. "Oh, I know."

"How?"

"Because I asked them to take you." He grew suddenly concerned. "They didn't hurt you, did they?"

"No. But they knocked me out with something."

He nodded. "But I did specify that they were not to hurt

you. Private security squads in North Korea aren't very professional."

"So they're mercenaries."

"Yes."

"And you hired them just to rescue me."

He shrugged. "They owe me a lot of favors."

She must've looked skeptical, or petrified, or both, because William mustered a kindly smile and hobbled over. He put a friendly hand on her shoulder. "This is a safe place for you, Ainsley. The regime can't touch you here. Trust me."

Ainsley felt herself relax. Her intuition told her that this man was telling the truth.

The paramilitary cowboy interrupted them with a quick sentence, and a gesture to the road. The old American answered him in fluent Korean.

"We should move inside," said William, "just in case prying eyes are out and about. We can talk freely in the living room."

He hobbled to the door of his home, pulled it open, and held it.

Drawing a deep breath, Ainsley entered the home.

Once inside, she looked around. William's home was plain. A low sofa, reading chair, repurposed coffee table. Wooden floorboards smooth with years of use. What seemed to be a piece of vintage farm equipment was standing propped against the wall. Except for the mid-sized television standing unplugged in the corner, the place was rustic enough to serve as a display window at a trendy lifestyle store.

William gestured to the sofa. "Make yourself comfortable."

Ainsley made her way over to it. Something about seeing such an ordinary piece of furniture drained the last remaining bit of strength from her legs. She barely made it to the cushions before they finally gave out.

From the kitchen, William said, "I know you have a hundred questions, but let's make sure you are healthy first."

He returned with two glasses, a small pitcher of water, and a bottle of clear liquid and placed everything on the low table.

Ainsley picked up the bottle.

"It's soju," he said.

She didn't know what soju was, but she was afraid to accept anything from this mysterious American. If he had the power to kidnap her, he had the power to do far worse.

"What is it?"

"Liquor."

"No, thank you."

He poured her a tall glass of water, then poured himself a glass of the liquor. He settled into his reading chair opposite her, resting his soju on top of his prodigious belly. "You really should try it. It's good."

"I can't believe that I'm looking at you right now," Ainsley said. "I mean, you're an American."

"Likewise," he replied. "If I sound a little weird, it's because I haven't spoken English for a long time."

"How long?"

"Decades."

"You sound normal."

"Really? No strange accent?"

"Nope." She refilled her water and regarded her host. "How do you know who I am, William?"

"Kenneth Park told me about you."

"You know Kenneth Park?"

He sipped his drink. "We've known each other for years."

Ainsley thought he was making their relationship sound too casual. As though it were no big deal for a Christian missionary to drop by on someone sequestered in a rural portion of the most closed, anti-religious society in the world.

"Then you know why I came here?" she asked.

He smiled. "You had a plan to find the famous onyx teacup."

The onyx teacup. He already knew about that. She sat back on the couch and held a hand to her forehead. "I have so many questions for you, I honestly don't even know where to begin."

"Well," he said, "it's usually easiest to start with the first one."

Ainsley thought about it. "I have three." She ticked them off on her fingers. "One, where am I? Two, why are you here? And three, what do you want from me?"

William leaned his head on the back of his chair and closed his eyes. "The answer to your first question is that you are in the village of Ujeobeo. You're about two hours outside of Pyongyang. It's been my home for years."

"So why are you here?"

He breathed out. "That's a long story that will be told later."

Ainsley nodded. "Okay."

"The answer to your third question." His eyes found her own. "I want to help you get the onyx teacup."

"You know about that?"

He smiled. "Of course. I even know where it is. And after you get it, I'm going to help you to escape the country."

William watched her reaction. Ainsley's heart leapt inside her chest. In the back of her mind had sat that very same nagging question: How to get out? After all, she'd most likely screwed her chances of a legal exit. The safest way to leave now was an illegal river crossing into China, the way thousands of desperate locals did every year.

"So what's the catch?" she said.

"We'll talk about that tomorrow," he replied.

She watched him casually sip his soju. The catch could be

anything. William didn't seem like a dirty old man, but you could never really tell. He had been living in the rural countryside, after all. Even in her present condition, Ainsley was probably the best thing he'd seen in years.

"Tonight, you're going to rest." He nodded towards the window. "We don't have much more time anyways."

Ainsley turned her head. The sunlight was slanting red into the room, and the first purple glimmering of twilight appearing behind the mountains to the west.

"What do you mean?"

"We live by to the sun here," he explained, "because the electricity is unreliable. If you don't believe me, look in my refrigerator."

Curiosity got the better of her. Ainsley managed to get to her feet, go to the kitchen, and open the small refrigerator. Inside was a stack of magazines and some glassware.

"It's empty. And warm."

"It's not even plugged in. Nobody has used refrigerators for years."

Ainsley remembered seeing a satellite photo of North Korea at night—a black spot on the map, unable to even light itself, surrounded by the bright lights of all the other Asian countries.

She looked at the elderly expat. William didn't seem particularly bothered by his reduction in lifestyle. He'd made his peace with it.

She made her way back to the sofa, poured herself a small glass of the soju, and held it in the air.

"To our homeland," she said.

His face brightened. "You've changed your mind. Good. My evening soju has been the only thing that's kept me sane."

He hoisted his drink up and they toasted the air. Then Ainsley threw the liquor down her throat. It was smooth and slightly sweeter than she'd expected.

"Not too bad," she said. "Kind of tastes like vodka."

"It's distilled from sweet potatoes. In Pyongyang they drink this stuff all night."

Ainsley felt her head beginning to swim. "I think I need to sleep."

"Of course."

She felt the side of her face fall onto the sofa. Then she felt the old man's thick fingers tucking a blanket across her shoulders.

This sleep wasn't from whatever they'd given her that afternoon. This was sheer and utter exhaustion. All it had taken was a single mouthful of liquor to push her over the edge.

Then Ainsley's eyes closed, and she didn't wake up for many hours.

CHAPTER THIRTY-TWO

Dawn.

Ainsley cracked open an eyelid. In front of her, a tray had been set out on the coffee table. On it lay a plate covered by a small dish towel. She lifted the towel. It covered a sizable helping of vegetables and rice.

Last night's dinner. She'd slept right through it.

At the sight of the food, Ainsley felt her stomach erupt. She'd gone nearly forty-eight hours, including running a marathon, without a proper meal.

She flung the towel aside and began shoveling the food into her mouth with her hands. William had provided chopsticks but she knew they wouldn't go fast enough.

After the massacre was finished, Ainsley wiped her hands and mouth on the towel and stood up. Her legs were still jelly, but they felt a little more solid than yesterday. Now they were like refrigerated jelly.

Her recovery had begun.

She stepped outside and squinted in the early sunrise. The sun was just cresting the eastern mountains and begun to bathe the valley in pale yellow light. The aroma of fresh herbs on the crisp air greeted her nostrils.

Before her, William was kneeling in the garden. He wore old gray clothing, worn out and crusted in dirt. In his hands was an ancient pair of rusted pruning shears. He was using them to trim back some of the ground cover.

"Good morning," he said.

"How long did I sleep?"

"I don't know," he said. "I haven't had a clock in years. There's tea on the table."

To the side of the patio stood a rough-hewn wooden table. A teapot and an empty cup awaited Ainsley. She filled it and stepped out into the garden, wriggling the dirt between her toes, feeling the chill of the night on her feet and the warmth of the day on her face.

"Are you ready to talk now?" she said.

"About what?"

"You. Why you're here."

He sat back on his haunches. "The story of my life could be made into a documentary. That is God's honest truth."

The sun grew higher as Ainsley listened to William speak of his childhood in Tennessee, his abandonment by his parents, his arrival at a foster home. How he'd run away from foster parents at age fourteen, enlisted in the army, married by nineteen, divorced at twenty-two.

"I was hopeless," he said. "I thought I was a loser. I hated myself."

"So what did you do?" said Ainsley.

"I asked the army to assign me to the South Korean DMZ. One day on patrol, I decided that I'd had enough of everything. I didn't have any family. I didn't have a wife. Even my friends had stopped writing me. I'd spent all my money on prostitutes. I had nothing to live for. That's when I decided to do it."

"Do what?"

"Walk across the border."

"Into North Korea?"

He nodded.

Ainsley took a seat on a nearby crate and listened as he continued the story. It was 1963, and while on patrol he had simply entered the DMZ, that tangle of wilderness and land mines, and begun to walk. It was madness, the most heavily fortified border in the world. He'd heard his fellow enlistees shouting at him in the distance. In response, he'd turned and shot at them with his rifle.

Ainsley was taken aback. She'd heard of people making life changes before, including herself, but never quite on a scale like this.

"So what did you think you were going to find here?" she said.

He pulled a carrot from the earth and brushed off the dirt. "I don't remember. It doesn't matter anyways. They captured and interrogated me. I convinced them that I wasn't a spy. After a couple of weeks, they gave me a choice."

"Which was?"

"I could be put on trial, or I could act in a movie."

Ainsley wasn't sure she'd heard that right. "Stand trial ... or act in a movie?"

"Yes."

"North Korea makes movies?"

"Of course. They used to make a lot of them, back when Kim Jong-il was alive. He was a movie fanatic. He built a powerful film commission and even kidnapped a South Korean actress and director. He forced them to remarry each other and then forced them to make propaganda films for him. They finally escaped during a trip to Austria." William stopped digging, his sad eyes on the horizon. "They were a nice couple. I liked working with them."

"So you appeared in a North Korean movie."

"No," he said, "I appeared in forty-three North Korean movies."

Ainsley started laughing. William Yaris was looking at her, bemused. "I know it sounds funny."

"It's not just funny," she said, "it's ridiculous. How did an American become a North Korean movie star?"

"I'll tell you how. They always needed a bad guy."

That made sense. "You were the only American they had."

"For a long time, there were four of us. But two died, and the third one couldn't act his way out of a paper bag. So they used me." William paused. "The third one eventually escaped too."

His chin tipped down. Ainsley could smell the heavy odor of regret clinging to him.

"So you ended up a favorite of the regime," she said.

He yanked a handful of radishes from the earth, then dumped them into the basket. "I was essentially a very odd pet. But it gave me a lot of advantages."

"You have a private security detail."

He laughed. "No, they're not mine. But they do what I ask because they know I used to carry weight in Pyongyang."

"Not anymore?"

The American shook his head. "No, not since Kim Jong-il died. I can't say that his son has been very pleased with me." He sat back on his knees. "It's been a good run, Ainsley, but my life is finished."

It was always sobering to hear someone say those words. Ainsley felt a rush of sympathy for the man. "You don't have any hope that you could leave?"

William Yaris looked at her calmly. "This country is where hope goes to die."

There didn't seem to be anything to say to that. Ainsley

studied her teacup as though it contained answers to life's greatest mysteries.

She cleared her throat. "So tell me where I can find the onyx teacup."

William hoisted himself to his knees and turned his bulky body towards her. "Well, you weren't going to find it in Pyongyang."

"So where is it?"

"It's here."

He was serious. Ainsley suddenly sat up straight. "In this house?"

"No," he said, then pointed to the mountain range. "Up there."

Ainsley got to her feet and looked at the range. The gentle slopes, the serrated peaks.

"How do you know it's there?" she said.

"I can't tell you that yet."

"Why?"

William lifted himself to his feet, hobbled over to her side, and took her hands in his own. She looked into his eyes. The small flame of life that burned within them seemed to have grown stronger.

"Because you have to promise me something first," he said.

Ainsley moistened her lips. "What is it?"

"When you escape to China, you have to take someone with you. Someone dear to me."

"Who?"

He nodded towards the house, and Ainsley followed his line of sight. A silhouetted figure had appeared in the doorway.

Then the figure stepped into the sunlight. It was a twelve-year-old girl.

"My daughter," he said.

CHAPTER THIRTY-THREE

Ainsley looked at the girl. She was tall and slender, with long black hair parted over her almond-shaped face. A pair of large, liquid blue eyes peered out curiously at the stranger in her garden.

As she moved into the sunlight, Ainsley sucked in her breath. She was astoundingly beautiful.

The girl came over to him, and he put a fatherly arm across her shoulders. "This is Kirina. She's lived in this village for her entire life."

"She's never left?"

He shook his head. "I don't allow it because people stare at her. Once, a group of women even tried to attack her."

"Why?"

"She's half white. Most North Koreans haven't seen a white person before."

Ainsley nodded. Racism went in every direction. "Who's her mother?"

He sighed. "A Japanese woman. The regime decided that I needed a wife, but they didn't want to allow my blood to pollute their own. So they kidnapped Tomoko from a beach in northern Japan and brought her here. We were married for six years."

"What happened to her?"

William's throat quivered, and he choked out the answer: "She escaped too. Seven years ago. I've raised Kirina myself since then."

Kirina. A gorgeous name for a gorgeous girl.

She set down her tea, feeling her legs still shaky beneath her. "William, with all due respect, I didn't ask you to kidnap me. I certainly didn't come here to play savior to anybody. All I wanted was to get the onyx and leave. That's all I'm going to do."

William nodded. "My daughter is the key to doing that."

"Why?"

"Because she's the only person who knows where the onyx teacup is."

Ainsley swung her gaze towards Kirina. The girl's expression was unreadable—distant yet close, intelligent, innocent, all at the same time.

"You have the onyx teacup?" she said.

The girl nodded. "I hid it in the mountains." Her English was halting but decent.

Ainsley was confused. "Wait wait wait. William, the teacup was here all along?"

William Yaris grinned. "Only for about two weeks. Kenneth gave it to me for safekeeping. But I told him that I didn't want to have it in the house. It's too valuable. I didn't even want to know its whereabouts in case the authorities questioned me."

Ainsley circled the girl. In a heartbeat, her mission had changed. Its success now depended upon a twelve-year-old shut-in with the face of an angel.

"I've been teaching her English for years," said William. "Ask her why she wants to leave the country."

"Kirina, why do you want to leave North Korea?"

It took a minute for the girl to summon the words. "Because my father says I will have a better life in another place."

That was for sure, thought Ainsley. This girl could be strutting down the runways of Paris draped in Givenchy.

"I don't want her living in these conditions," said William. "The average salary used to be three dollars a month. Now it's a dollar fifty. You can make better money picking up loose coal on the sides of the roads."

"So you're saying this girl's future depends on me," said Ainsley.

"Yes."

Ainsley touched a weary hand to her forehead. Her original plan had officially been blown to smithereens. Now she was being forced to accept a substitute plan that was decidedly more humanitarian. Even worse, she didn't seem to have any choice in the matter—not if she had any ambitions beyond subsistence farming in disguise for the rest of her days.

William had begun to rake his garden. "You've been asking so many questions, Ainsley, I think it's my turn to ask you one."

"Okay," she said.

"How were you planning to smuggle the onyx teacup out of the country?"

"By covering it in clay." She quickly explained the process that the church had recommended to her.

He looked surprised. "They told you to do that?"

"Yes. I practiced it a few times."

William shook his head. "You would've been dead meat. Kenneth and I talked about it. Better that it didn't work."

The truth dawned on Ainsley. "So it was you and Kenneth who changed the plan."

He yawned. "Maybe."

"Now I can see you're an actor," she said. "That's exactly what you did. That's also why he handed me that little note. To get me here."

William grew slightly defensive. "It was in everyone's best interest. Including yours. Ainsley, all this regime knows is security. That's it. There's literally nothing else they're good at. They can't feed the people anymore. They've lost our respect, especially in the northern cities."

"But—"

He continued. "The regime even asked the city people to make toibee this winter. Do you know what that is?"

"No."

"It's when you mix your own shit with ash and dry it in the open air until the spring."

Ainsley gulped. "That is disgusting."

William Yaris threw down the rake. He was growing angrier.

"This used to be an industrial nation. There was an explicit contract with the people. The government controlled the food and gave everybody their rations." He snorted. "Now they've broken that contract. Let's eat two meals a day. Can you believe that? Why do you think I live out here in the country?" The old man swung his arm around the vegetable garden. "Everybody grows their own food now. If you don't, you die." He pointed a finger at Ainsley. "And you might've died too, if you'd tried to take out that onyx teacup covered in clay."

Ainsley thought back to Pastor Jeong. "Do you think the minister in the U.S. was lying to me?"

"I don't know. At the very least, he was ignorant about the regime. Maybe he believes he knows more than he does."

That was possible. Pastor Jeong didn't have the boots-on-the-ground information that William and Kenneth had.

But what if there had been bad intent?

Despite the morning sun, Ainsley felt a chill go up her spine. It was possible that Pastor Jeong wasn't who he said he was. It was possible that she'd been set up by the churchgoers to be arrested by North Korean police. Her mind reeled at the thought. She spun it around, looked at it from all angles, but it still didn't make sense. Who would benefit from that? An American woman arrested for smuggling a gemstone out of the most closed society on earth? Sure, it would've been a mildly compelling story. Maybe the television would've turned her into another media sensation. But who would've profited from that?

She was stumped.

Ainsley's reverie was interrupted by a loud rapping on the front door of the house.

William's eyes flew towards the door. "Oh, crap."

"Who is it?" said Ainsley.

"The *inminban*. They're neighborhood busybodies. They keep tabs on everybody and report back to the state." He tapped Kirina on her shoulder. "Take Miss Ainsley into your room. Don't come out unless I tell you. And be quiet."

Kirina moved inside, gliding without a sound. Ainsley followed close behind, the floorboards squeaking under her feet.

They entered the girl's bedroom. It was simple—a woven mat, a low bed, a smattering of Korean-language books. Kirina quietly closed the door and they sat down cross-legged on the mat. The girl lifted a finger to her lips. Ainsley nodded. In the other room, William was speaking in low but rapid Korean. A woman's voice barked short phrases in response.

With nothing else to do, Ainsley sat quietly and looked at her thumbs. They were ordinary thumbs. They'd lived ordinary lives back home. It was oddly reassuring to see them accompanying her here.

She looked up. Kirina was studying her. Ainsley managed a smile. The girl responded with a smile of her own that revealed, in the middle of the exquisite face, two rows of gray teeth. Ainsley blanched. The girl was too young to look like that. It would be fixed when they made it to China.

If they made it China.

The conversation in the next room ended. The front door clicked shut.

Kirina was on her feet in a shot. She ran out into the main room, Ainsley following.

William had sat down on the edge of the sofa. He looked worried.

"What happened?" said Ainsley.

"That was Mrs. Lee. She's the worst one." He glanced at Ainsley wryly. "Putting their noses in other people's business is the favorite pastime of middle-aged Korean women. Especially in Ujeobeo."

"Did she know I was here?"

"Not until she saw those."

He pointed at Ainsley's pink-and-white trainers on the floor. Ainsley felt a wave of panic grip her system. She'd forgotten to hide them.

"I tried to lie that they belonged to Kirina. She didn't believe me. Now she's suspicious because we didn't register anybody as a guest."

"You're supposed to register guests in your own house?"

William nodded. "It's mandatory for all overnight visitors. Name, gender, registration number, travel permit, all that."

Ainsley collapsed on the sofa. "So now what do we do?"

"I promised to begin attending the *hakseup*."

"What's that?"

"They're weekly meetings. I stopped going years ago. They just sing the same stupid patriotic songs."

"And what about me?"

He fixed her with an intense gaze. "I don't know if you're going to be safe here. Those women will be back, and soon."

Ainsley sat on the floor and slumped against the wall. All because of her shoes.

"Tonight," he continued, "you'll follow Kirina into the mountains. She'll lead you to the onyx teacup."

Ainsley sighed. "I'm still recuperating from the marathon, William."

The old man shook his head. "You don't have a choice, Ainsley. I'll put together some provisions for you."

CHAPTER THIRTY-FOUR

As the long gray shadows disappeared into the total darkness, Ainsley followed the twelve-year-old girl, keeping her head down behind a hedge.

On Ainsley's back was a small hand-woven rucksack. Inside were two bowls of rice and a sauce made of ground red bean paste, mixed with chopped zucchini. William had decided against adding kimchi because the smell would be too sharp for two people traveling in secret.

That afternoon, William had explained how the northern cities had suffered the most during the famine. Starting in the nineteen seventies, a caste system had grown in North Korea, one that was every bit as rigid as the one that existed in India. A person's level was determined by family; the sins of the father literally became the sins of the son. Over time, the poorer, more "impure" families had been pushed out of Pyongyang and out of the warmer southern land. Those outcasts ended up migrating the cold northern cities, and when the famine hit, the regime cut off rations to those areas first. That's where the famine hit hardest, with people dying in the streets and bands of orphans robbing anything that moved.

Ainsley chewed all this over in her mind as they moved swiftly out of the village of Ujeobeo, passing through a gate marked by two stacks of cuboid blocks. Ainsley recognized them. William had told her that afternoon that they'd been designed for defense. If the village were ever under attack, the military would knock the cubes into the road.

Soon the dirt village gave way to a field. The grass felt springy under her feet. Ainsley glanced into the sky. Tonight was a full moon, providing nearly enough light to see by.

That wasn't good.

Kirina led her along the edge of the meadow and into a grove of small trees. The girl reached up to a branch and plucked something and handed it to Ainsley. It was hard and firm and round.

An apple.

Ainsley looked around. They were standing in a small apple orchard.

"An apple is good to eat," whispered the girl.

"That's true," said Ainsley.

Kirina plucked another and took a bite. Then she spun around in happy circles, dancing to some music in her head.

Ainsley watched her. She was as innocent, and as pure, as a person could be here.

"I want to know about life in your country," the girl said.

Ainsley chewed the apple. "What do you want to know?"

The girl thought about it. "Is it true that you can make a cake?"

Ainsley smiled. "Sure."

"Every day?"

"If you want to."

A faraway look appeared in the girl's eye. "I want to do that someday."

"We'll bake one together," said Ainsley. "It's not hard."

The girl brightened up. "I would like that."

Ainsley picked six more apples and put them into her sack. "How much further is the onyx?"

Kirina pointed towards the dark wall. "It's up there."

"How do we get there?"

"There is a way."

"Is it difficult to climb?"

The girl shrugged. Something about her easy attitude raised Ainsley's suspicions, but she forced herself to lower her defenses. This girl was otherworldly.

"Kirina," she said, "I want you to know that I'm trusting you. That's a big responsibility."

The girl avoided her eyes. "I trust you too."

For the next three hours, the two women moved through the landscape, the undergrowth crunching beneath their shoes. Ainsley found herself imitating her guide, moving as lightly as possible across the leaves and dirt.

The two ghosts floated to the right side of the sheer wall, flew up into a narrow gully, drifted around a field of rocks, and emerged onto a trail. It was lined by pines and ran along a narrow knife's edge of rock.

Ainsley and Kirina followed it, twisting around the curves, dipping down into gulches, cresting low rises. All without a word.

After three hours, they stopped and uncorked the water bottle that William had given them before leaving. Ainsley drank from it and looked out at the landscape. The full moon had risen higher in the dark sky, bathing the plain below in a ghostly wash. The village of Ujeobeo was barely visible as a cluster of tiny structures.

"You're going slow," said the girl.

"Kirina, I ran a marathon yesterday."

"So you are very tired."

"Yes, I'm exhausted."

The girl took a few steps off the trail, got down on her knees beneath a tree, and began to dig in the dirt. There was an audible crack as her hands snapped something.

She stood up and offered Ainsley a long red stalk.

"Rhubarb," she said.

"For what?"

"You eat it and it gives you energy."

Ainsley smiled. "Thank you."

She broke off a piece with her teeth and chewed the root. It was bitter but she forced herself to swallow. It probably was good for the bowels too, but this really wasn't the time or place to be encouraging that.

Ainsley stowed away the water and the rhubarb and willed herself forward. She followed the girl as they continued picking their way along the now-stony trail in the moonlight. The night air was fragrant with the scent of trees.

At last they arrived at a small promontory. Kirina stepped off the trail and threaded her way through the trees towards the very lip of the cliff. Ainsley followed, feeling the rough, curling bark of birch trees scrape her shoulders.

At the edge of the cliff stood a single tree.

A spruce.

"This is the place," she said.

"Can I help you find it?" said Ainsley.

"No."

The twelve-year-old scampered beneath the lowest branches of the spruce and began to scamper up the trunk. As she disappeared into its foliage, the arms of the tree shook. There was an unbearable moment during which Ainsley clenched her hands so tightly that her nails dug little marks in her palms.

"Kirina?"

"I found it," came the girl's voice.

Ainsley felt elated. She noticed that her body was shaking. It might've been from the anticipation of recovering the teacup. It could've been from the anticipation of getting the hell out of North Korea. It could've been involuntary muscle spasms. Or all three.

"Uh oh," said Kirina.

Ainsley's forehead creased. "What?"

"Someone is coming."

CHAPTER THIRTY-FIVE

Ainsley felt a long talon of fear slice her open from chin to navel. She looked down the trail.

She couldn't see anything, but as she listened, she could hear distant sounds. People grunting, boots stomping. It wasn't just one person either. This sounded like a pack of men.

Ainsley ran back to the spruce. Kirina was still up in its branches, cloaked.

"You have to hide," the girl said.

"Where?"

"There."

Her arm came out of the foliage. It was pointing at another spruce. "That one can hold you."

From the trail, the voices were growing louder. Ainsley had to make a decision. She hadn't climbed a tree in decades. The only other solution was to run, which was not an option at all.

Quickly, she gripped the lowest branch with her left hand, another with her right, and pulled herself up. The soles of her shoes went sideways as they gripped the trunk. She used her thighs to push herself further up.

A moment later, she was three meters off the ground, encased in a partial screen of needles.

"Catch," said Kirina.

Ainsley looked over. In the nearby tree, the girl's arm was throwing something underhanded at her.

She saw the object sailing towards her, dark and glittering in the night air.

The onyx teacup.

She reached out. The object struck Ainsley in the palm—

—and bounced out of her grasp.

It fell onto the ground. She saw it bounce in the dirt below her.

Ainsley cursed the girl under her breath. This wasn't the time for games.

In no time at all, she'd scrambled down the trunk. Her feet landed on the dirt with a thump.

She picked up the gemstone treasure. It was surprisingly small, and really did fit neatly inside her hand, the way Pastor Jeong had predicted. She stuffed it into the pocket of her top and zipped it shut.

She listened closely. Behind the sound of tramping feet, something heavy was squeaking.

The men were coming closer.

A male voice shouted in the darkness, and the white beam of a flashlight suddenly shone in Ainsley's eyes, blinding her.

She lifted her hands to shield her face. "What do you want?"

The voice answered sharply. She didn't recognize the sounds it was making. With the white light in her eyes, she couldn't read lips either.

Then Ainsley felt a hand roughly grab her arm. She

instantly yanked it away. There was a flurry of movement, and she found herself in a headlock.

Ainsley struggled, flailing her arms, windmilling them. It made no difference. Her captor was strong. His strange body odor assaulted her nose and nearly made her retch.

She couldn't blame Kirina for this. A twelve-year-old girl raised inside a protected bubble had no idea of the consequences of her actions. To her, she'd just been innocently tossing a teacup.

Now Ainsley was caught.

Then she felt a stirring in the air. A lithe figure slipped between her and the other men.

It was Kirina.

As the flashlights landed upon the girl, the men murmured and backed away.

The twelve-year-old pointed her finger, swung it around, and said something in a loud voice. It wasn't the Korean language. It seemed to be the same gobbledygook that the men were speaking.

A man replied. Kirina answered. The men laughed.

Then Ainsley felt the muscular arm release her. She stood up and backed away fast, rubbing her neck. Her captor was a short, stocky man. He looked at her and grunted.

Ainsley looked at Kirina. "Who are these men?"

"Chinese merchants. They go down this path almost every night."

"Where?"

"They're going to Pyongyang. They go through these mountains so nobody sees them."

The girl said something to the men. The flashlight swung away and strafed across the group. Each was holding a large handcart that was teetering with piles of clothing, coffeemakers, lamps. Ainsley peered closely. There was a stack of Chicago Bulls jerseys.

Chinese merchants smuggling Western athletic apparel to North Koreans. This was too weird for words.

Ainsley's attention snapped back to the men. She noticed one looking at Kirina with a certain expression that Ainsley knew well. It was that predatory look that men get after too many days out in the bush.

She threw her arm across the girl's shoulders. "We should go."

"Okay."

Kirina waved goodbye. The two women began walking back down the trail, the way that they had come.

A minute later, Ainsley glanced back. She could see the traders, still watching them.

The only thing that had saved them was the fact that the men were tired. They were hauling merchandise in handcarts across a mountain range, after all.

Ainsley felt the onyx teacup in her pocket and felt a surge of energy. She was ready to escape the country now.

And William Yaris was going to help her.

CHAPTER THIRTY-SIX

The pair returned to Ujeobeo just before dawn. They passed the same gate of cubes, slunk behind the same hedge.

"Hurry up," said Ainsley, "before somebody sees us."

As they approached the road to William's house, she caught sight of something far up ahead. A crowd of people.

"What's happening?" she said.

"I don't know," said Kirina.

A short whistle caught Ainsley's ear. She turned her head. There was a familiar van parked just off the road. Behind the wheel was the paramilitary cowboy.

They crossed the street. The man popped out of the vehicle, slid open the backseat door, and gestured to enter. He seemed agitated.

"Can we trust him?" said Ainsley.

"He's friends with my father," said Kirina.

"I don't even know his name."

"It's Dae-woo."

"And your father trusted him enough to bring me here from the capital."

That was enough. Ainsley climbed into the backseat of the van, Kirina following. They pulled the door shut.

In the driver's seat, the paramilitary cowboy twisted around and began to explain something rapidly. Ainsley noticed the liquor on his breath as he pointed down the road, towards William's house.

"What's he saying?" said Ainsley.

Kirina's voice was very small. "He says that my father went away. He says it's dangerous to go to the house."

"Where did your father go?"

The girl translated the question, and Dae-woo grew quiet. Then he muttered something.

"He doesn't know."

"Did he go alone?"

Another pause. The man answered quickly, as though it embarrassed him to say it.

A look of shock passed across Kirina's face. She didn't say anything.

"Tell me," said Ainsley.

"Somebody took him."

"Who?"

The girl's eyes were wide. "The *inminban*."

That was the local village organization, headed by the woman who'd entered the house yesterday. She'd seen Ainsley's shoes on the floor.

Maybe it was related. Ainsley felt her heart thump harder against her chest.

Dae-woo blurted something else. His finger pointed to William's house down the road. His eyes were a pair of small, frightened animals cowering in his skull.

"We can't go home," said Kirina. "He says they're waiting for us."

The paramilitary cowboy started up the van. Ainsley felt herself start to panic. All the feelings from the black market in Pyongyang came flooding back to her. She clutched Kirina's hand.

"Where is he taking us?" she said.

"To his house until my father returns," replied Kirina.

The driver barked something else.

"He says we have to lay down so that the people don't see us."

The two females flattened themselves against the seat. Ainsley remembered being in this same position, headbagged and wristbound, two days earlier.

The van pulled into the road. It jounced down the rutted road, the shocks squeaking in pain. Ainsley felt her body lift up and crash down.

Ten minutes later, the van stopped.

"*Seodulleo*," said Dae-woo. In English: *Hurry up*.

The door slid open. Ainsley and Kirina slipped out of the van. They were standing in a road on the edge of the village. In front of them was a harmonica house, the humble and basic two-room unit that dominated rural housing.

"Let's go inside," said Kirina.

"Fast," added Ainsley, "before someone sees us."

As they ran to the house, the front door opened. Kirina kicked off her shoes and carried them inside. Ainsley did likewise.

Inside the door stood Dae-woo's wife. She twisted the hem of her sleeve between nervous fingers.

The paramilitary cowboy followed them inside, then shut the door. He explained something in Korean.

"He said we're safe here," said Kirina.

Ainsley looked around. The kitchen was in the main entry room. A hearth stained black meant they burned coal to cook. A portrait of the latest Kim hung on the wall, a meticulously folded towel on a side table below it. A sliding door separated the kitchen from the main room.

Ainsley walked to the window and peered outside. Instantly she felt the woman's hand pulling at her arm, her voice jabbering.

"She says we can't go near the windows," said Kirina.

The wife gestured to a mat in the center of the room. Ainsley knew an order when she saw one. She obediently sat herself on the mat. Kirina sat next to her.

Dae-woo walked out the door and closed it behind him. Ainsley heard the van's engine turn over and pull away.

Kirina and Ainsley sat quietly while the woman went to the kitchen and scooped something onto two small plates. She brought them over.

"*Gomabseubnida*," said Ainsley. In English: *Thank you*.

The woman watched as Ainsley sliced off a piece of cake with the fork. It was light gray and very dry. She placed it in her mouth.

"What type of cake is this?" Ainsley asked.

Kirina translated, and the woman responded.

"It's tree bark," said Kirina. "She learned how to make it into a powder during the famine."

Ainsley forced her eyebrows back down onto her face. "Kirina, the cake we'll make together will be even better than this."

Kirina's eyes lit up in excitement. Meanwhile, Ainsley looked around for a napkin. There wasn't one. Instead, she leaned over to the side table, took the meticulously folded towel, and wiped her mouth with it.

Dae-woo's wife suddenly shrieked, her face a mask of agony. Ainsley froze.

The woman leapt to her feet and snatched the handkerchief from Ainsley's hand. Then she rushed to the kitchen, talking to herself.

Kirina looked embarrassed.

"What just happened?" said Ainsley.

"That cloth is only supposed to clean the picture of Dear Leader," she said. "If the *inminban* sees that the cloth is dirty, she will be in trouble."

Ainsley looked at the portrait, at the smiling face, scrubbed skin, and gelled hair. He was one of the most inhumane and transparently hypocritical leaders in the world, and yet there was a special cloth just to clean his image.

She glanced in the kitchen. The woman was furiously scrubbing the cloth in a pot of water.

"Does the *inminban* inspect all the houses?" she said.

The girl shrugged. "It depends if they like you or not."

Ainsley sat down next to her. "So they don't like your father right now."

"The old regime liked him. The new regime doesn't care about him."

"Where do you think he went?"

"I don't know. Sometimes he disappears for a day or two."

"He never tells you where he goes?"

Kirina shook her head.

Ainsley lapsed into silence. She sat cross-legged on the floor, listening to the small clicks and scrapes of the trees outside the window.

An hour passed like that. Then another. Then another. Ainsley pulled her knees up to her chest, set her forehead against them, and shut her eyes. She was exhausted but didn't want to move. She might disturb something in the house.

Next to her, Kirina hummed quietly as her fingers toyed with the edge of her shirt. Ainsley knew that behavior. The girl was trying to find her happy place.

Meanwhile, the lady of the house was reading a book in the corner. Ainsley squinted at the cover, trying to make out the title. She recognized the characters spelling the English word wind.

"Kirina, how do you say the name of that book in English?" she said.

The girl looked over. "*Gone With The Wind.*"

"By Margaret Mitchell?"

"Yes," said Kirina.

Ainsley attempted to process this. She couldn't. It was too weird.

A few minutes later, she'd slumped over on her side and fallen asleep on the mat. Kirina laid down alongside her and soon was asleep as well.

———

Four hours later, the sound of the van outside the house woke them up.

The front door opened, then slammed shut. Dae-woo entered the house like a fierce warrior. His face was dark and strained. Under his arm was a plain wooden box, crusted with dirt.

Ainsley stood. Kirina did too. She faced the paramilitary cowboy and asked a question. He ignored her. She asked again. He ignored again.

She asked a third time. He whirled.

His eyes were rimmed with red. He held Kirina's hands in his own and spoke intensely. Ainsley didn't catch all of it, but she watched the girl's eyes. First they widened, then they went disbelief—and then the tears began to fall.

Those tears Ainsley told everything that she needed to know.

William Yaris wasn't coming back.

CHAPTER THIRTY-SEVEN

The three of them sat together around a low table in the second room. On the tabletop were three chipped porcelain cups filled with tea.

Ainsley had one arm around Kirina's slim back. She could feel the girl shaking.

On the girl's lap was the box.

Dae-woo had just explained what had happened while they'd been sleeping.

He'd gone to William Yaris' house. He'd found five members of the *inminban* there, including Mrs. Lee. She'd ordered William to be taken away in an official van under the charge of harboring overnight guests without permission.

His voice had faltered as he'd said this, but Kirina had stayed unusually strong. It occurred to Ainsley that William had probably prepared her for this day.

Dae-woo said that he'd waited until all five members of the *inminban* had left. Then he'd sneaked into the backyard and quickly begun digging in the dirt in the place where William had instructed him. That's where he'd found the box.

The last gift from William Yaris to his daughter.

"*Yeol-eo*," he said. In English: Open it.

The girl hesitated, then swung the lid open. Everyone craned their heads to look inside.

There were two envelopes and a note.

Kirina unfolded the note. It had been written in English.

My daughter,

Enclosed are two envelopes. One envelope, with the won, is for Dae-woo. He will use this money to get you to the river. The other envelope, with the yuan, is for you. Take this money with you and use it after you cross into China. Be sure to avoid Dandong. It's crawling with agents of the regime and if they catch you they will send you back here. Look for the church people; they will help you get to Seoul.

When I am released, I will find you.

Appa

Ainsley felt a tear spring to her eye. William had known exactly what awaited him. He'd prepared all this ahead of time.

Kirina peeked into one of the envelopes. It contained the Korean currency. She handed it to Dae-woo. He inspected the cash, then grunted. He seemed satisfied.

Ainsley looked into the other envelope. She counted at least ten thousand yuan. She didn't know the exchange rate but figured that had to be a lot of money.

Underneath the envelopes was one more item.

A knife.

It was a fixed-blade combat weapon, about five inches

long. The bottom half of the blade was serrated, which meant it could be used to cut many different materials.

She weighed it in her hand. This could prove to be very valuable.

"I'm going to carry everything," she said, "as well as the yuan."

"Okay," said Kirina.

"Ask Dae-woo when we should leave."

The girl translated, and Dae-woo grew very serious. His index finger stabbed the table. Ainsley understood that without any help. *Tonight*.

"*Eodie?*" said Ainsley. In English: *To where?*

"Yalu," said the man.

The Yalu River. Separating North Korea from China. The best, and only, way to sneak out of the country.

Dae-woo looked to his wife. The woman went to the kitchen and began to put together a meal. As they sat at the table, sipping more tea, they discussed where William might have been taken.

Dae-woo described the three levels of North Korean prison. First was a detention center operated by a low-level police unit. Second was a labor camp whose prisoners stayed for a month or two at most. The most severe punishment was the *kwanliso*, the colony of labor camps in the northern mountains. This is where the worst criminals were taken— Christian collaborators, Japanese collaborators, rival politicians, those who read foreign newspapers, those who cracked jokes about the regime, and all living members of the criminal's family. Spouses were off the hook as long as they got divorced. Almost nobody ever made it out of *kwanliso* alive.

"Which one do you think William has gone to?" said Ainsley.

Dae-woo shrugged his shoulders.

She looked at Kirina. "I hope your father goes to the first one."

"Me too," said the girl, her lip quivering. Ainsley held her a little closer.

The wife arrived at the table with three small bowls of rice and a plate of what seemed to be white mushrooms. Daewoo's eyes lit up. These were apparently delicacies.

They quickly downed the food. Ainsley looked for a second helping. There wasn't any. She remembered the apples in her rucksack but decided to save them for later.

She had a feeling that she would need all the energy she could get.

CHAPTER THIRTY-EIGHT

As the last glow of purple evaporated from the sky, Dae-woo opened the front door.

It was time to leave.

Ainsley stood behind him. She fingered the onyx teacup in her pocket. She'd been holding it for almost twenty-four hours. It almost seemed like an afterthought by now.

In her rucksack were the apples. Nothing else. She hoped to find some food along the way.

She and Kirina moved quickly into the backseat of the van. Dae-woo closed the door after them, then slipped behind the wheel and started up the engine.

The van pulled along the row of harmonica houses and onto the main road. It turned away from the village.

Then Dae-woo hit the brakes. Ainsley looked ahead.

In the road ahead, the cuboid blocks had been pushed over. A military truck was parked alongside it. It was a roadblock.

"*Eop deu ryu*," he said. In English: *Get down*.

Ainsley and Kirina flattened themselves in the backseat. Dae-woo quickly threw a blanket over them.

The van pulled up to the roadblock. An official had already stepped to the edge of the dirt track. Ainsley listened to him chatting with one of the officers.

Then Ainsley felt the van turn in reverse, back around, and return the way they'd come.

She lifted her head. Dae-woo looked back at her and said, "*Hakseup*."

Ainsley remembered William mentioning that word. Kirina described it further. Every Tuesday evening, an indoctrination session was held in cities, towns, and villages across the nation. On that night, North Koreans gather in public to read and recite the statements of Dear Leader. They sing patriotic songs. Everything closes, including the black markets. Nobody answers their phones. It's a mandatory public meeting.

"So it's mandatory," said Ainsley. "That's no big deal. We'll just wait in the car and leave after."

The girl translated to Dae-woo. His face had twisted itself into a strange grimace, but he said nothing.

They took a short road back into the village. The van's headlights strafed across people walking in twos and threes alongside an irrigation ditch. They wore pitiful clothing— grayish brown and dirty, mere suggestions of shape. Their backs were hunched like pitiful question marks. Their gaits suggested a lifetime of pain.

This was the reality of North Korea.

As the van drew towards the center of the village, Ainsley saw four klieg lights that had been set up in a clearing. The lights were attached to a generator, which in turn was connected to a car that was running with its hood open. The people were standing in loose clumps, hands thrust into pockets, waiting.

Dae-woo stayed a safe distance from the lights. He parked the van in the shadows. About ten meters away, Ainsley spotted a metal handle and spigot poking out of the side of the muddy road. It was the village water pump.

He turned around and said something quickly to Kirina. Then she looked at Ainsley. "He said that we should stay here."

"That's what I suggest," she replied.

Dae-woo exited the van. They watched him slosh away through the mud towards the klieg lights, a silhouette in cowboy boots.

The pair sat there, waiting in the dark van.

"It's stuffy in here," said Ainsley.

"What is stuffy?" said Kirina.

"Hot."

Ainsley rolled down her window and felt the cool night air sweep in across her face. It was a relief. This country was spiritually suffocating. Back home, she sometimes found herself getting upset when the person in front of her at a green light didn't accelerate fast enough. She felt ashamed of that now. It was clear how lucky she had been to have been born in a free society.

Outside the van, a group of voices drew her attention. Three women had arrived at the water pump, dark shapes carrying buckets. One began vigorously pump the handle, priming it, until the water gushed out. They took turns filling their buckets.

As the women chatted with one another, Kirina sat still, listening. Ainsley did too, but without any context, it sounded like gibberish. There was no program in the world that could prepare someone for the harsh accents and spat syllables of spoken peasant language in rural North Korea.

Then she heard them say a familiar word.

Wi-yam-nom.

The first two syllables were William. The third syllable, *nom*, meant *the bastard*.

They were talking about Kirina's father, and not in a good way.

The girl instantly stiffened. Ainsley barely dared to breathe. The women were growing more agitated now, gesturing to the klieg lights. One woman spat a particularly nasty sentence.

Kirina suddenly cried out.

Ainsley covered the girl's mouth with one hand and rolled up her window with the other.

"You have to be quiet," she said.

Kirina's body was full-on shaking, her eyes gone wild. Ainsley could see her hyperventilating. The girl was suffering a full-fledged panic attack.

"No!" Kirina said. "They can't! I have to—"

The girl twisted out of her grasp, threw open her door, and climbed out of the van. Ainsley lunged over the seat, trying to catch the girl by the shirt, but Kirina was too fast. A moment later, she was out of the van and running towards the lights.

Ainsley sat there in the car, trying to understand what had just happened. The girl had overreacted to something she heard. This was normal for preteens. But that interpretation didn't hold much water. The way she'd been raised, Kirina wouldn't know what a spoiled hissy fit was.

No, those women had said that something terrible was about to occur.

Ainsley knew her decision: She would bring the girl back to the car before it could happen.

She slipped out of the vehicle and crept towards the middle of the village.

CHAPTER THIRTY-NINE

In the darkness, Ainsley skulked along the edge of the settlement, feeling the cold wet muck squelch under her feet.

As she approached the circle of light, she stayed low and kept to the shadows. She found a large bale of straw, about the height of a person, and crouched herself behind it. She peeked around the edge and watched the scene.

The townspeople of Ujeobeo had formed a ring around a cement pole, around which the klieg lights were centered. A cable ran from the lights to the open hood of a nearby vehicle, whose motor was running. There was even a television crew nearby, their single camera on a tripod, recording the proceedings. Ainsley guessed that it was for the state news channel.

Something was about to go down.

Then she felt a hand grip her arm. It was Dae-woo, intensity burning in his eyes.

"Kirina," whispered Ainsley. Then she pointed towards the lights.

He barked something that sounded like a curse word. Ainsley could tell that he was upset by the news.

A noise drew their attention. In the center of the circle, a short woman in a prim black dress with shoulder pads stood with a microphone. An ancient speaker behind her emitted a sibilant hiss. Her lips were puckered into a tiny sphincter of hate.

Ainsley didn't need a formal introduction to know who that woman was. Her looks said everything. It was the leader of the *inminbam*.

She began speaking. Given such a bad microphone, Ainsley couldn't make out any of her words, except one.

Wi-yam-nom.

William the bastard.

She said it three times in under a minute. The crowd was silent.

Then all heads turned as two men brought in a hooded man. He was heavy and waddled with a certain sadness. They removed the hood, and suddenly the sad blue eyes were blinking and looked out at the assembly.

William Yaris.

His official captors guided him over to the post and produced a length of rope. Ainsley watched as they walked in slow circles, winding the rope around both man and pillar. Tinny patriotic music echoed from the small PA system. After seven circuits, William had been tied securely to the pillar. He held his head high and fixed his resigned eyes on the dark unknown horizon.

Ainsley realized what was happening.

They were going to kill him.

A small, choked whimper caught Ainsley's ear. It was Kirina, not more than ten meters away, in the dark. She was crouched down in the mud, her hands held to her head.

"Dae-woo," whispered Ainsley.

She nodded towards the girl. Recognition dawned on his face. He pulled a length of fabric out of his pocket, wrapped it in his hand, and strode through the mud to where William's daughter was hiding.

Ainsley watched as he put his arms around the girl, whispered something in her ear, then quickly tied the fabric around her mouth. She was gagged. Then he wrapped the cloth around her eyes as well. Kirina tried to resist with feeble kicks, but they were useless.

Soon Dae-woo was dragging the girl through the mud, away from the event, back towards the van parked in the darkness.

Ainsley watched them pass. She made no effort to reach out to the girl. It was better to get her away quickly from whatever was about to happen.

Dae-woo shouted at her. Ainsley didn't respond.

Something told her stay behind the hay bale.

Ahead, a man stepped into the circle of klieg lights. He was wearing the official state uniform of olive green with red trim.

Strapped to his body was what appeared to be a leaf blower. A pack on his back was connected to a long tube in his hand. Ainsley wondered why anybody would need something like that here.

Then she saw a flash of orange at the tip of the tube. That wasn't a leaf blower.

It was a flamethrower.

The state official stepped a few paces away from William, then turned to face him. Ainsley felt every muscle in her body tense. She should do something. She needed to rescue him.

The prim woman swung her finger around to the people, making get-back motions with her hand. The crowd shuffled backwards a few paces. Then she pointed at the people standing behind the pillar. They quickly dispersed.

The state official assumed a wide stance. He pointed the

long tube at William. The elderly American looked up into the sky and closed his eyes.

A massive tongue of fire licked out of the tube. Ainsley instinctively jerked back and clapped her hands over her face.

The flame disappeared as quickly as it had appeared. Two seconds, at most, but it had hit William in the torso. She could see the smoke rising off his shirt. His head had lolled to the side and his mouth had fallen open. Then Ainsley heard it.

He was moaning.

Ainsley felt her guts wrenching themselves into a hard little ball. Her eyes scanned the scene. There had to be some weapon she could use. A length of wire. She would garrote the state official.

Then she remembered the knife in her backpack. It was in the van.

Before she could act, the orange flame shot out of the weapon again. This time it stayed on.

William Yaris was bathed in a cloak of fire. Ainsley crouched behind the hay bale, rooted in horror as she watched it consume his body. His clothing evaporated. Then his skin cracked, blackened.

Ten, fifteen, twenty seconds.

His subcutaneous fat reached its boiling point, and the skin began to slough off the body in flakes and sheets.

Twenty, twenty-five, thirty seconds.

There were two pops in his skull. Those were his eyeballs. They'd boiled and burst.

Then the flame disappeared, and the state official lowered the weapon. The rope had been burned away, and William's body fell over onto the ground with a thump.

Ainsley stuck her hand in her mouth to keep from retching. She felt like somebody had just reached into her chest cavity and ripped out her soul.

Then she heard something.

Another moan.

William was still alive.

The spectators remained silent. This man had been their neighbor, and nobody moved. The state official walked towards the mutilated body. Stood directly over it, pointed the weapon a third time. Then blasted another stream of fire. He held it for twenty more seconds.

The smell of cooking flesh reached Ainsley's nose—

And she finally fled.

Crying, she streaked back to the van, her feet barely touching the mud, and threw herself into the backseat and slammed the door behind her. Kirina was in the back, still bound at the eyes and the mouth, her body wracked by sobs. She'd heard enough to know.

Dae-woo was at the steering wheel, smoking calmly.

"Let's go," she said. "Now!"

He didn't need a translation to understand. He started the engine, turned the van around, and drove them away from the center of the village.

Ainsley untied the binding on Kirina's face. Then she took the girl in her arms and lay down on the back bench with her and held her as she cried and screamed and thrashed.

An hour later, as the van rumbled on, Kirina finally fell into unconsciousness. Ainsley stayed awake, holding her, stroking her hair, until the village of Ujeobeo was a distant memory behind them.

CHAPTER FORTY

The next morning, chin in palm, Ainsley stared morosely out the window of the van at the passing scenery.

It was brown farmland, broken only occasionally by a windbreak of trees.

Next to her sat Kirina, the girl's knees hitched up to her chin and her arms wrapped tightly around them. She was staring out the window mutely. She hadn't said a word for hours. She'd entered a state of shock. This girl was going to need help, but there wasn't exactly a therapist on call here.

Ainsley placed her hand onto the girl's. There was no movement, no response, no sign of life. She kept her hand there anyways.

"Kirina," she said, "can you ask the drive how much longer?"

The girl said a string of syllables.

The driver wiped his face in that way that very tired people do. "*Dandongggaji han sigan gyul reo.*"

Kirina looked straight ahead. "He says one hour to Dandong."

Alarm bells went off in her head. She shook Kirina's arm.

"Tell him we can't go to Dandong. Your dad says—said—it was dangerous."

The girl translated, and Dae-woo answered with another long stream of rapid Korean.

"He said he is only the driver," said Kirina. "He's going to drop us off with another man who will help us cross the river."

"What is the other man's name?"

Kirina translated. The driver shrugged, then explained something briefly. "He says it's probably a fake name so there's no point in telling it."

Now the alarm bells were ringing even more loudly. Ainsley calmed herself down, forced herself to lower her expectations. By definition, illegal border crossing wasn't neat, tidy, clean, or safe. She'd just have to accept that.

She turned her attention to the passing scenery again. A hulking gray communist-bloc factory appeared on the right side of the road. The windows had all been broken and the doors were missing. As they passed, Ainsley could see that the vast interior had been emptied too. It was a shell of a facility.

This was just one of the thousands of empty factories she'd read about. Anything that could be stripped from the dead industrial sector had been stripped—copper, rubber, metal. It was a land of garbage pickers. She felt even more worry gnawing at her stomach.

Another half-hour, and twenty more gutted factories passed by the window. Ainsley grew impatient. She also began to become aware of a particular stench in the vehicle. It was bothering her.

"Do you smell that?" she said.

Kirina looked over at her. "What?"

"I don't know. It's something gross."

The faintest hint of a smile cracked at the edges of the young girl's lips. "I think it's you."

Ainsley lifted the edge of her long-sleeved wicking jogger's top and put her nose into the space. Instantly she pulled her nose out and crossed her arms.

"You're right," said Ainsley.

Kirina started giggling, at first softly, then more loudly. It was contagious. Ainsley felt the uncontrollable giggles rising up in her too.

Before long, they were both wracked with heaves of laughter that rose up out of their souls like something that couldn't be contained any longer.

DANDONG

CHAPTER FORTY-ONE

As the van crested a small rise, Ainsley looked through the windshield and felt her spirit lift.

Spread before her was a broad, murky river, and on the other side of its waters lay China.

Freedom.

Or something like it. The word was relative.

Stretching across the river was a modern four-lane trestle bridge. Dae-woo explained that it was the New Yalu River Bridge, designed by China at a cost of $350 million, and wasn't yet finished because North Korea hadn't yet compensated China for its part.

On the other end of the bridge, on the other side of the river, was the city of Dandong, China. After a week of seeing nothing but gray drudgery, Ainsley's eyes feasted upon the modernity. New condominium towers. A busy cargo port. A string of brightly colored lights that festooned the balustrade on its riverwalk. She could even see neon signs hanging over the distant supermarkets. She imagined the long aisles of food.

But that was there—and she was here. There was no

crossing that bridge, not for a young North Korean like Kirina, and not for an American without a passport either.

Their crossing would be different.

As they approached the sad border city of Sinuiju—the broken-down sister to the glamour across the river—Dae-woo cranked the steering wheel to the right. Soon the rickety van was putting along the four-lane road that ran parallel with the river. Outside the windows, the road was lined with one- and two-story cement block structures that were the color of old sludge. Here and there a cold smokestack poked out of the top of roofs. It felt barren and bleak. Everything seemed as though it'd been empty for a generation.

Ainsley felt her spirit sink again.

The van pulled into a warren of nondescript industrial sheds and rolled through the dirt to the rear of the compound, where there stood a tall fence protected with razor wire. A rolling gate was the only way in, and standing at that gate was a thin, mean-looking man. A cigarette hung from the corner of his mouth.

Dae-woo parked and stepped out. He exchanged a few words with the man, who nodded, then rolled open the gate.

The paramilitary cowboy returned to the van and opened the side door. "*Geu nam ja dda ra ga.*" Ainsley understood that. In English: *You go with him.*

Kirina stepped out of the van, Ainsley right behind. The girl hugged Dae-woo. He tolerated it, his face impassive.

Ainsley gently pulled the girl away from the driver. Then she put out her other hand.

"Thank you," she said.

He ignored her hand but gave her a quick bow of the head. She replied with the same. Then Dae-woo climbed into the van and pulled away.

Ainsley and Kirina walked into the compound, and the smuggler rolled the gate shut behind them.

———

Ainsley stood inside the empty manufacturing facility, faintly disgusted.

It felt like an abandoned abattoir. The concrete floor lay barren except for a dirty mattress flung along the far wall. The only items in the room were the drain, a ventilator fan, and a dirty mattress.

Ainsley crinkled her nose. It was the type of room seen in the finale of a bad thriller.

The smuggler swaggered into the room, cigarette still hanging from his lip. His shoulders were hunched over in an angry posture and his feet fell heavily on the concrete.

He leaned his shoulder blades against the wall and took the cigarette out of his mouth. When he looked at the two women, his eyes were two knife slits in his face.

Ainsley whispered to Kirina. "Translate for me." She raised her voice. "What's your name?"

Kirina translated. The man didn't reply. There would be no answer to that question.

"When do we leave?" said Ainsley.

"Tonight," said the man.

"Where will you take us?"

"Forty kilometers north."

"Why?"

"That's where the border security is weakest."

That made sense. Ainsley decided to push it a little bit. "After we cross over, what should we do?"

"Don't trust anybody," said the smuggler. "There are many North Korean agents on the other side. The only ones you can trust are the ones who tell you the password."

"What's the password?"

"Night swallow."

Ainsley guessed that it referred to the time that most emigrants made the crossing.

"So now we wait?" she said.

"Yes."

The smuggler tossed the cigarette on the ground, stubbed it under his shoe, then walked out. The door clanged behind him.

Ainsley leaned against the wall, then slid down until her rear had touched the ground. Kirina sat next to her and put her head on Ainsley's shoulder.

"I miss my dad," she said.

"I miss him too," said Ainsley, "but remember that he wanted this for you."

"Yeah."

They didn't say anything for a while. Ainsley listened to the dripping of a distant water tap somewhere.

"I don't like waiting," said Kirina.

"You can go to sleep. I'll stay up."

Kirina leaned her head on Ainsley's shoulder and slowly shut her eyes. Ainsley exhaled and felt her body relax.

Hurry up and wait.

She didn't notice when sleep crept up behind her and closed her eyes too.

CHAPTER FORTY-TWO

Hours later, leaning sideways against the wall, Ainsley was fast asleep.

She was deep in one of her weird dreams. She was running across a field of marshmallows. Behind her were strange monkey-like creatures, giant vicious puppets, and their huge mouths were sucking up everything from the ground behind her. Ainsley knew that they were trying to devour her too, but she couldn't resist stuffing marshmallow plants into her mouth. Then, just as the creature snagged her by the heels—

A small whimper reached her ears. Ainsley jerked back into consciousness.

When she opened her eyes, she saw something horrific.

Across the room, the man was on the mattress. Beneath him was Kirina. He had one hand covering her mouth while the other one was beginning to rip open her pants.

Ainsley leapt to her feet. In half a heartbeat, she ran over to the mattress and grabbed the man under the arms and hauled him off the girl. She heard a voice cursing him out in furious English. It took a while before she realized that it was her own.

Then she stood there, breathing, while he looked up at her from the floor with total hatred. She kicked at him. He crawled away like a malevolent insect, then pulled himself up to his feet. He spat on the floor at Ainsley's feet. Then he limped out the door. It clanged shut behind him once again.

Ainsley stood there, breathing heavily, hands on her hips. Then she looked down at the girl.

"Are you okay, sweetie?"

"Yes," said Kirina.

"Are you sure?"

"I'm sure," she said. Then she looked up at Ainsley. "What was he trying to do?"

Ainsley felt her heart soften a little. This girl had been so sheltered that she didn't even quite understand her own value in the sexual marketplace. William had protected his daughter extremely well, but soon Kirina would learn the ways of the world.

"He was going to rape you."

Kirina looked confused. "What's rape?"

"I'll explain it to you as we walk," said Ainsley. She extended her hand and helped the girl to her feet.

She looked at Ainsley oddly. "Where are we going?"

"To the crossing." Ainsley fixed her with a serious stare. "We can't stay here, Kirina. That man is going to come back, maybe with some friends, and then things will get a lot worse. For both of us."

Kirina seemed to understand. "He said it was forty kilometers north."

"Tie your shoes," said Ainsley. "It's going to be a long night."

———

They left the warehouse and rolled the gate aside and exited the compound. They stood in the dirt for a moment. Kirina started to turn back up towards the road, but Ainsley caught her by the arm.

"Not that way," she said, "there's too much traffic."

They looked around. Ainsley spotted, across a small field, the barest outlines of a railroad track. It was heading parallel with the river.

"Let's follow that," she said, pointing.

The pair quickly scurried away from the warehouse complex. They skirted a pile of concrete blocks, crossed under a thin line of barbed wire, and finally emerged upon the railroad track. They turned right and began to follow it north.

As they walked, the crushed-stone ballast crunched beneath their feet. Ainsley guessed that this track had been laid half a century earlier, when the country still expected economic success.

Ainsley looked at the sun. It was nearing the horizon, no more than an hour of light left. This wasn't as bad as it seemed. In the daytime, she and Kirina were sitting ducks for the regime's guards patrolling the river. In the darkness, they had a chance to avoid detection.

She stuffed her hands into her pockets, feeling the onyx teacup. Ainsley had been going so hard, for so many days, that she'd continually forgotten that it was even there. Yet it was the reason for this insanity.

Now here she was, trudging along a railroad bed in rural northern Asia, an illegal in an outlaw nation. One step away from being tossed into a concentration camp and flayed alive with tenterhooks.

Her eyes glanced to the left. She recognized the gap in the landscape. It was the river, about half a kilometer away. Safety lay on the other side. All they needed to do was survive until nightfall, then walk quietly over.

She spotted a guard tower along the river's flank. A pointed roof peeking above the rough weeds. It was no taller than a lifeguard tower at the beach.

Then a dog barked.

Ainsley froze. That didn't sound too far away. It could easily be a guard dog.

Her gut told her exactly what to do. She grasped Kirina's hand. "Let's get down. We should hide in the bushes."

"Okay," said the girl.

They descended from the elevated railroad and ran down the shoulder of the track and plunged into the high bushes that surrounded either side of the ties. Ainsley led the girl a few meters into the thick brush. Then they stopped.

Ainsley heard feet on rocks. Someone was walking down the railroad shoulder.

Kirina's eyes grew wide. Ainsley lifted a finger to her lips, then drew the girl in close. They stood huddled together, barely daring to breath.

The footsteps crunched louder. Ainsley could hear an animal, its lungs occasionally forcing a brusque snort. She peered through the greenery. She caught a glimpse of olive-green fabric, the red rim around the comically broad olive-green hat.

An official sentry.

She shrank down a little further and lowered her head, praying that the dog hadn't picked up their scent.

Then the crunching stopped. The guard was standing on the railway tie directly in front of their hiding position. The dog was sniffing hard. Ainsley lowered her face to her chest.

Then the guard moved along.

Ainsley's body crumpled. She gave thanks to whatever god existed in the heavens above for an old dog, an impatient sentry, whatever.

They waited five minutes, ten minutes. The guard didn't come back.

"How long do we stay here?" said Kirina.

"At least until dark."

"What should we do?"

She looked at the girl, and a smile crinkled her mouth. "We're going to bake."

CHAPTER FORTY-THREE

As the sky turned from blue to purple to black, Ainsley and Kirina were crouched deep in the bushes, making mud pies.

Digging into the ground with her fingers, Ainsley'd described how, in her country, people made cakes with wheat flour, which you bought in a bag. That had blown Kirina's mind. The only flour in Ujeobeo was nut flour, and the people ground it by hand with a mortar and pestle. Ainsley then described the other ingredients that went into a cake—eggs, butter, sugar. She didn't mention vanilla extract and grated orange peel.

"And then, after you've mixed them together," Ainsley explained, "you pour them into a pan."

"How big is the pan?"

"Well, there are many different sizes," she said, "but personally I prefer a bundt pan."

"Why?"

"Because it's hollow in the middle. It cooks faster and it keeps you from eating too much."

From the girl's confused look, she knew she'd just mangled

something again. Then she realized her error. In North Korea, there was no such thing as eating too much.

Ainsley dug her hands into the mud and began shaping it into a round little cake. She relished the squishy feeling of the stuff between her fingers. It felt weirdly therapeutic.

Kirina began shaping her own little mud pie. "I want to bake a cake."

"I already promised you that we'll make one together."

The girl looked up at her. Ainsley took a moment to study the girl's face. It was young, true, but already there were traces of hardness beginning to line the edges of her eyes.

"You know, I lost my father too," Ainsley said.

The girl's face fell. Ainsley wanted to thunk herself in the head for having killed the good mood.

"He died of cancer," she continued, "when I was your age."

"Do you miss him?"

"All the time," said Ainsley. "We used to travel together. Sometimes I can feel him with me when I'm exploring."

The girl was openly gazing at her, her eyes wide and trusting. Ainsley felt the sudden violent urge to grab her by the shoulders, tell her how goddamned beautiful she was, tell her to never change, and don't let anybody change you either, stay just like this for as long as you can, because this innocence is the best thing you'll ever have.

But she didn't.

"I love my dad," said Kirina.

"He was a good man," replied Ainsley, careful to use the past tense. "You're going to be a living testament to him."

"What does that mean?"

Ainsley forced herself to speak more simply. "It means that wherever you go, your actions will reflect him. Because he made you."

Kirina understood that. "So I'm going to be a good person like him?"

"Exactly. And you're going to be strong, because your dad was really strong. Especially when we cross the border."

"He went to a new country, and so am I."

"Good point."

They spent another minute patting their cakes, discussing how they would eat them, from which direction, whether or not there would be powdered sugar on the outside, what kind of tea to drink with it.

When they couldn't see the ground anymore, and the chill had begun to rise up their feet and into their legs, Ainsley knew it was time to go.

"Let's move," she said. "But no talking. Do you understand?"

The girl shook her head yes.

"Okay—quietly now."

They slipped out of the undergrowth and went back to the tracks.

———

For most of the night, the two crept slowly northward along the railroad tracks, their shoes crunching on the ballast of the railroad track.

Twice more they had to dive into the undergrowth and wait for the sentries that strolled the railway to pass. Ainsley discovered that you could spot them coming by the orange tip of their cigarettes in the darkness.

At one point, her stomach let out a long, loud, plaintive growl. She understood its complaint. The apples were long gone. She would need to find food soon, even if it meant scavenging for berries or eating grass.

Her feet were killing her too. She thought about how long

they'd been walking—about six hours, by her estimate. She knew that the typical human usually walks five kilometers per hour, but they'd been walking a little faster, maybe six or seven. That would put them at about thirty-six to forty-two kilometers.

That meant they'd probably reached the crossing point.

She looked to the left. Though all was darkness beyond the edge of the brush, Ainsley had that distinct feeling that they were near the river. There was a certain humidity in the air, a liquid presence flowing just beneath the surface of perception.

"Are we there yet?" said Kirina.

"I think so," said Ainsley.

She had to admire the way the girl had kept up, especially after the horrific event in her village. Preadolescents weren't exactly known for their love of forced marches, but Kirina had tolerated this one well.

"So how do we get to the river?"

"Your guess is as good as mine," replied Ainsley. "Maybe if I put you on my shoulders, you can see."

They stopped. As the quiet hum of insects rose out of the undergrowth, Ainsley crouched down on one knee. Kirina climbed onto her shoulders. Unsteadily, Ainsley rose to her feet.

"What do you see?"

"I think it's right there," said Kirina.

"How far?"

"Maybe a hundred meters."

"Through the undergrowth?"

"Yeah, and it looks really thick."

Ainsley lowered down to her knee, and the girl leaped off her shoulders. Then a tiny sound in the distance sent a shiver of terror up Ainsley's legs. It was the sound of an engine, and it was coming from behind them.

She looked back. Far down the railroad tracks, a single white light was slowly heading towards them.

"Is that a train?" said Kirina.

"No," said Ainsley, "it's something else."

She peered more closely. On either side of the vehicle, beams of white lights strafed the undergrowth. They were searching for something.

Ainsley felt her heart leap out of her chest. "Into the bushes!" she said, grabbing Kirina by the arm. "Go! Now!"

CHAPTER FORTY-FOUR

The pair ran into the undergrowth. Ainsley pushed a few steps into the tangle but found her way blocked by boxwoods. They were tough to penetrate.

"We're going to have to force our way through this," she said.

"Can I help?" said Kirina.

"No. Just stand back."

Ainsley looked up. The white light coming down the track was growing larger.

With her forearms up to protect her face, Ainsley barreled hard into the undergrowth. She had enough velocity to crash a few meters, the branches rebuking her legs with vicious slaps. Then she slowed to a stop.

"Stay close to me," she called to Kirina. "We're going to have to cut our way through."

Ainsley whipped off her bag and reached inside for the combat blade that William had left them. He'd known what she would need. All too well.

She put the knife in her good right hand, then raised her arm and used it to cut at the branch in front of her face. It took four or five hacks to get to the point where she could twist it around and bend it down, allowing passage. She was thankful for the serrated teeth.

Two steps forward, and Ainsley hit another branch. She worked on this one the same way. The third time, the girl reached forward and did the twisting and breaking. Working together, they repeated the process for the next fifty meters or so—Ainsley hacking, then Kirina twisting.

All the while, they could hear the vehicle drawing nearer, even as they plunged deeper into the brush.

"Hurry," said Ainsley.

"I'm hurrying," said Kirina.

Finally, the engine grew so loud that Ainsley had to turn and look. They were about forty meters into the undergrowth now, but if she stood on her tiptoes, she could see the vehicle over the top of the greenery.

It appeared to be a motorcycle, riding between the rails. The white light was now sweeping in crazy arcs on both sides of the railroad. It occasionally glanced off a hand grip, a mirror, a gear box.

The motorcycle arrived at the point where Ainsley and Kirina had plunged into the brush. Its roving light crossed one another—

—and then stopped. It stayed fixed on the broken opening in the bushes.

Then the engine shut off.

Ainsley clenched her fists and mouthed a silent obscenity. This couldn't be happening.

"Whoever it is," she whispered, "has just found us."

"We can't go anywhere," said Kirina.

"I know." Ainsley looked around. "All we can do is stand to the side and hope he doesn't see us."

The two girls pushed about two meters to the left before getting blocked by another tangle of thick boxwood branches. Ainsley steeled herself. This couldn't be the end, not when they were so close.

"Stand behind me," said Ainsley. "Don't move until I tell you to."

Ainsley hid her right hand behind her back—the hand holding the knife. It was pointing straight down. Kirina squeezed in behind her.

She heard the pursuer crashing through the path that they'd cleared. Ainsley felt the sweat popping out of her skin. The knife grew hot and slippery in her hand. She had no idea if she had the fortitude to use it.

The crunching footsteps grew louder, the first flicker of light shone on the branches.

Then the man came crashing through the brush, and the flashlight was upon them. Ainsley stiffened, barely daring to breathe. She couldn't see anything with the light in her eyes.

He said something. She didn't understand the words, but she recognized the voice. It was the smuggler, the one they'd run away from. He'd pursued them all the way up here. There had to be a good reason.

"*Yeogiwa*," he said. She knew that term. It meant *come here*.

"*Ani*," she said. *No.*

He repeated the command, this time more harshly.

Ainsley put her right foot slightly forward, flexing her fingers and toes. All her muscles were tensed.

She repeated her response again.

The man took a step forward towards them—

—and before she could react, Ainsley felt the knife get pulled out of her hand.

Quick as a snake, Kirina darted around her, took two quick steps towards the smuggler—

—and plunged the knife into his thigh.

The man howled with pain. He lashed out, trying to grab the knife. Kirina pulled it out, sidestepped him, then neatly drew the blade across his palm. A line of red appeared on his hand and dripped like a thin ribbon of red crepe paper.

"Go!" shouted Kirina.

The man was hopping on one leg to keep his weight off his bleeding thigh.

"Go!" she shouted again.

The man spat at her, then lurched his way back down the corridor through the broken bushes. A minute later, Ainsley heard him struggling to start his motorcycle. At last it roared to life, and it disappeared back down the railroad track. Ainsley didn't know how long a man with two bleeding knife wounds could expect to control a motorcycle on a railroad track, but that wasn't her problem.

Ainsley stared at Kirina in amazement. "You are full of surprises."

The fire that blazed in the girl's eyes was even stronger than the one that had consumed her father.

"I want to leave this country," the girl said.

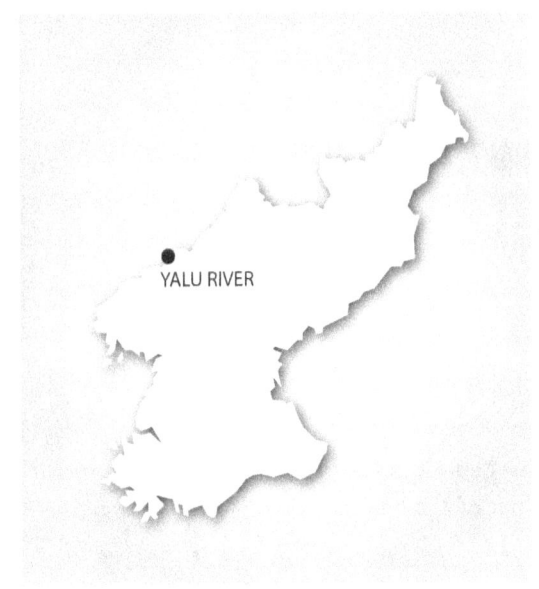
YALU RIVER

CHAPTER FORTY-FIVE

An hour later, in the darkest hour before dawn, the two women finally broke out of the bushes and found themselves on the riverbank.

The Yalu River.

Because their eyes had adjusted to the darkness, Ainsley could see how narrow the river truly was. The opposite bank appeared to be no more than a long stone's throw away, fifty meters at most. Given the flatness of the terrain, she doubted the water would ever be more than hip deep.

Fifty meters to freedom.

The crossing looked easy. Ainsley had forded rivers like this as a girl. It was surprising that this little trickle was all that separated the people of North Korea from new and better lives.

But there were other things to consider.

Kirina bent down and began scooping water into her mouth. Ainsley did likewise, plunging her hand into the water. It instantly went numb. The river was frigid. That was something to consider.

They both drank their fill. Then Ainsley stood up. "Kirina, you look north, and I'll look south. Watch and listen for guards."

"Okay."

They stood back to back, eyes focused on the long stretch of riverbank in opposite directions. Ainsley felt her limbs beginning to tremble as the cold of the river crept into her body.

"I see one," said Kirina.

Ainsley turned quickly. The girl was pointing at a tiny orange dot standing out brightly in the darkness.

"That's probably a guard tower," said Ainsley.

"How far away is that?"

"Close enough to shoot us."

They didn't say anything for a moment. Ainsley added: "But remember—he can't shoot us if he can't see us."

Kirina nodded. "So we have go before the sun comes up."

"Right away. There's no point in waiting."

Ainsley began to strip off her clothing. "We have to go naked so that our clothes stay dry. This way, we stay warm when we reach the other side."

Kirina lowered her head in modesty. Ainsley put a hand on her shoulder. "Don't worry, I won't be able to see you."

"Okay."

The girl slowly peeled off her shirt and pants. She wasn't wearing a bra, didn't need one yet. Ainsley was surprised, however, to see the girl sporting a dainty pair of pink-and-white underwear. She wondered how she'd found those in that godforsaken little village.

"Keep your shoes on," said Ainsley. "If it's rocky, you'll need them to walk. And you don't want to fall in this water."

A moment later, the two women had stripped themselves naked except for their shoes. Ainsley rolled up their clothing into a tight little ball, put it in the knapsack, closed the draw-string, and slung it onto her back.

They faced the river, side by side, already shivering. "We should hold hands," said Ainsley, "in case one of us stumbles."

Kirina's hand crept into hers and gripped it tightly.

"One, two..."

"...three," the girl finished.

They stepped forward into the water. It was ankle deep. Ainsley felt her feet go numb. "Oh my God!"

Kirina let out a little shriek. "It hurts!"

"No more talking. Let's move."

They began to pick their way across the river. The bottom was rocky, and Ainsley struggled to find footing between the large, rounded stones lodged on the floor of the river. The icy water slowly crept higher, up to her knees, like the fingers of the grim reaper.

"My feet are hurting," said Kirina.

"Keep going," ordered Ainsley.

As they reached the middle of the river, the current grew stronger, pressuring Ainsley's knees sideways. Kirina's thin legs wobbled violently with every step. At last, she let go of Ainsley's hand and began to windmill her arms, her torso lurching around crazily.

"Careful!" said Ainsley.

It was too late. The girl disappeared with a splash into the current.

"Kirina!" she shouted.

A moment later, Ainsley saw the girl's head bob above the surface, watched her arms splash about. She could see that Kirina was trying to find her footing—

—but the current began to sweep her downstream. Ainsley gasped. The longer the current carried the girl, the more momentum she would pick up, and the harder it would be for Kirina to stop herself.

Then Ainsley realized something else, something much more horrifying.

The girl didn't know how swim. She'd had no opportunity, not living in that wretched little village.

That meant that she needed to be rescued.

Ainsley took a breath and dove headfirst into the water. It was instant agony. Inside her chest, her lungs began convulsing like a pair of writhing eels. She broke the surface, gasping, spluttering for air, pawing at the water.

She forced herself to continue swimming, but paddling became difficult. It felt as though someone had injected frozen gel into her rotator cuffs. She felt panic spreading through her body but willed herself to stay calm.

A few interminable seconds later, she'd caught up with Kirina. The girl had given up struggling against the current and had let herself be carried. She weighed next to nothing, had not an ounce of fat to protect her from the cold water.

Ainsley grabbed the girl's arm. Her head jerked up, and in the first crack of predawn light, Ainsley saw on her face that sleepy, unfocused look of someone who'd been on the path towards death.

"Get on your feet," said Ainsley.

The water was still hip deep here, and Ainsley struggled to find her own footing in the powerful current sluicing around her body.

Meanwhile, the girl hadn't moved. Her eyes were closed. It seemed that she'd passed out.

Ainsley knew her task. She would have to tow the girl the rest of the way to shore.

She hooked her left arm across Kirina's bare chest and put her hand into the girl's right armpit. That was supposed to be one of the warmest parts of the human body, but hers was cold to the touch. The girl's head fell backwards into the small of Ainsley's neck.

Ainsley's lips tightened. She was determined not to let the girl die like this, so close to escape.

She pushed herself backwards into the water and began an elementary backstroke, her legs making powerful frog kicks under the icy water, her right arm pushing the water, while her left arm stayed wrapped around the unconscious girl's chest. She gritted her teeth in pain. Her limbs felt as though they'd been filled with sludge.

At last Ainsley felt her heel bang a rock. She tested the depth. The water was shallow here, less than thigh deep.

With great effort, she drew both herself and the unconscious girl up to a standing position, her arm still wrapped around Kirina's chest.

The bank was only a few meters away. Just a few more strides. Her wet body, exposed to the cold air, began to convulse. She knew the risk of hypothermia was real.

With painful slowness, she pulled Kirina through the water, the unconscious girl's heels dragging on the river bottom. Ainsley felt the pain deep in her bones. Each step felt as though someone were swinging a wrecking ball into her thighs.

At last she stepped onto the riverbank. She looked down at her sodden running shoes. She couldn't feel their texture. Inside, her feet were frozen solid.

She lay Kirina down in the dirt and kneeled next to her and pressed her ear to the girl's sternum. The girl's heartbeat was there, slow but strong. Her lips were slightly pale.

Ainsley quickly unslung the pack from her back and opened the drawstring and dumped out their clothing. It was soaking wet. That was expected.

Quickly she spread out the clothing on a nearby bush and prayed that it would dry quickly.

Her body hadn't stopped its violent shivering. And Kirina hadn't regained consciousness. They were in dire need of a blanket. She spun around, looking for something, anything, to use for cover.

Down the river was a small dead tree, a smattering of dead leaves still clinging to the branches. Knife in hand, Ainsley picked her way down the riverbank. She hacked at a couple of large branches, then twisted them off.

She carried the branches back to the unconscious girl. Kirina opened her eyes. "I'm really cold," she said. "What happened?"

"You almost died and I saved you."

The girl regarded her. "Thank you."

"You're welcome. Now take off your shoes."

The girl obeyed. Ainsley did so as well. It felt like pulling shoes off a mannequin. She could've driven a nail through them without a twitch.

"Now roll over on your side."

The girl obeyed. Ainsley laid down in the dirt next to her, at the edge of the river. She brought the girl's backside towards her own front side until they were spooning.

"I know this is weird," she said, "but this is the only way we can survive until our clothing dries."

She wrapped one arm around the girl and used the other to draw the branches over themselves. Ainsley didn't know how effective this would be, but it was the best she could do. The sun would be up shortly.

The left side of her face on the cold ground, she exhaled on the girl's neck. She felt a thin film of wet heat already forming between her chest and the girl's back.

"Ainsley," she said.

"What?"

"You don't smell bad anymore."

A smile cracked the corner of Ainsley's mouth. The thought made her forget the horrible truth—that, at this moment, they were two illegal refugees laying naked and shivering together on a riverbank in remote northern China.

"Thank you," she replied.

"I want my front side warm now," said Kirina.

The girl turned over to face Ainsley. They pressed their bodies together, cheek to cheek, chest to chest, hip to hip, and waited for dawn to arrive.

CHAPTER FORTY-SIX

An hour later, Ainsley cracked open an eye. Her hands and feet were still cold, but her core temperature had risen almost back to normal.

She pulled her head back and looked at the girl. Kirina had fallen asleep with the right side of her face in the mud. Ainsley envied her. She was the type of person who could snooze with her head jammed beneath the seat of a public bus, as though it were the most natural thing in the world.

She gently disentangled herself from the embrace and stood up. The landscape had revealed itself in an eerie reddish-gray light of the strange morning sun.

Behind them was a fence.

That hadn't been visible in the dark. Ainsley looked at it. It was a chain link fence, about three meters tall, with three rows of barbed wire stretching horizontally along the top. She saw that it extended up and down the length of the river, as far as the eye could see.

Welcome to China.

No matter. She wasn't too concerned. Other people had

escaped this way before. If they walked far enough, there had to be a way over it.

Ainsley went over to their clothing. Only an hour, and it'd already dried beautifully. She silently thanked her lucky stars for having worn running gear on this pursuit. It'd been designed for easy wicking.

She donned her clothing and immediately felt better. She reached into the pocket of her top and felt for the onyx teacup. It was still there, hard and rounded. She would inspect it later tonight, once they'd found safety.

Then she squatted next to Kirina and gently shook the girl. "Your clothing is dry."

Ainsley helped the girl to her feet and watched as she put her shapeless North Korean garments over her slim figure. The clothing situation would be remedied soon. China was a consumerist paradise. All they had to do was find a town or city.

"Let's put on our shoes and get out of here," said Ainsley.

The two women dropped to the ground and began to slip them on. Ainsley put on her left shoe. She was reaching for the right one when a sharp crack sounded on the other side of the river.

The dirt exploded next to her, showering her in a small hailstorm of pebbles.

She instantly rolled out of the way, covering her head, then looked across the river. An official sentry was standing in full olive-green regalia on the riverbank, aiming his rifle at them.

The mouth of the weapon cracked again, and the ground next to Kirina exploded.

"Run!" shouted Ainsley.

The women scrambled to their feet, Ainsley still holding her right shoe in her hand. Ducking their heads, the women fled downriver, splashing through the ankle-deep shallows. Another crack sounded. The water exploded at Ainsley's feet, and she leapt out of the river like a flying fish.

"Where are we going?" shouted Kirina.

"Over the fence!" said Ainsley. "Can you find a way?"

Another crack. A tree branch exploded above their heads and came crashing down. Ainsley caught it and shunted it aside.

"I see a place!" said Kirina.

"Where?"

"Down there!"

Ainsley followed the girl's finger. She was pointing ahead to a short segment of the fence, about twenty meters further on, that appeared to have been cut down by previous escapees.

They ran behind the trunk of a nearby tree. Kirina was breathing hard.

Ainsley looked at the fence. Someone had used shears to cut a vertical line from the top of the fence halfway down, then peeled it sideways like a V. All she needed to do was make a running start, plant one foot in the saddle, hoist her other leg over, and jump down into the weeds on the other side.

Ainsley felt a surge of confidence. She'd been a track star once upon a time. She'd even run hurdles, though they hadn't been her best event.

She could do this.

She looked back at the shooter. He'd followed them along the river and was reloading. Even worse, he'd been joined by two other sentire.

Shit.

"What do we do?" said Kirina.

"If we stay here, we're dead."

"So let's jump over the fence."

Ainsley nodded. "I'll go first."

"No," said Kirina.

Ainsley placed her hands on the girl's shoulders. "You stay so I can help you on the other side."

She was still holding her right shoe in her hand. No time to put it on. Ainsley took a deep breath, then burst out from behind the tree.

Sprinting fifteen paces towards the gap—

—she heard the rifle cracks, the bullets popping all around her—

—and vaulted herself as high as possible. Her left foot landed in the cradle of the ripped portion of the fence. In one fluid movement she brought her right foot up and through the gap.

Then she was falling through the air on the other side of the fence. When she landed in the weeds, she felt an incredible pain explode in her right foot.

It was so intense that she fell over sideways on the ground, mouth open, gasping. Nothing came out. It felt as though she'd been impaled upon a pitchfork.

"What happened?" shouted Kirina.

Ainsley's felt something hard and metallic under her foot. She looked down. It was a long strip of iron spikes, each one about a centimeter high.

And it'd plunged directly into the sole of her bare foot.

She cursed out loud. The Chinese government didn't want North Korean refugees, and this fence, and now this strip, was their way of signaling it. She wondered how many refugees had been injured this way.

She pushed aside the strip of spikes, which were tipped red with her blood. Then she motioned to Kirina, on the other side of the fence. The girl burst out running from behind the tree.

Instantly, a flurry of cracks sounded from the other bank. A volley of bullets began falling around the streaking girl.

Kirina leapt into the split fence, then stopped. Her foot was stuck.

"Jump up!" said Ainsley.

"I can't!"

The girl was a sitting duck up there. Ainsley leapt up from the weeds on her good foot, reached through the gap in the fence, and dislodged Kirina's foot. Then she grabbed the girl by the armpits, hauled her through the fence, and lowered her down into the high weeds.

They lay there for a moment, breathing. The rifle cracks stopped. Ainsley looked over. The three sentries had lowered their weapons and were leaving the riverbank.

The girl's eyes fell upon Ainsley's foot. "What happened?"

Ainsley lifted up the sole of her foot. It was a disgusting bloody smear, two ripped holes in the flesh. She pointed at the nearby strip of spikes. "That happened, goddammit."

"Can you walk?"

"I have to," said Ainsley.

"Wait." The girl found a hole in the sleeve of her shirt and began ripping it.

"No—" said Ainsley.

The protest fell upon deaf ears. A moment later, Kirina had completely ripped off her own sleeve. Then she crouched at Ainsley's foot, wiped off the blood, then tied it around the foot, bandaging the wound.

Then she felt the girl's arm around her back, and then the girl's slim figure helping to lift her to her feet. As Ainsley placed pressure on the foot, her face winced with the pain.

"It hurts," she said, "but let's get moving before it gets worse."

"Where do we go?"

Ainsley shrugged. "We find someone to help us." She managed a grin. "This is the easy part."

They limped off, away from the river, arms around one another.

CHAPTER FORTY-SEVEN

The women crossed the eerie reddish-gray landscape for the next two hours. It was barren land, dotted with scrub brush and the occasional copse of trees.

She was in China.

All her life, Ainsley had imagined elaborate temples, calligraphy, chopsticks. Part of her knew those images were clichés. Modern China was exactly that—modern. She'd already seen Dandong from a short distance, and it had looked pretty much like Miami.

This part of China was no-man's-land, however.

Ainsley limped on, hoping to encounter a person, a road, anything to indicate a sign of civilization. Her foot was throbbing. Next to her, Kirina had gone totally silent.

Then the girl pointed. "I see something."

Ainsley squinted. Far off, maybe a kilometer away, a vehicle was moving across the scrubland.

"That's a road," said Ainsley.

Then she felt her leg buckle beneath her and fell onto the dirt. Kirina picked her up by the armpit.

"You can't stop," she said.

"I wasn't intending to," said Ainsley. "It just happened."

The girl helped Ainsley across the fields until they arrived at the shoulder of a two-lane asphalt road. A minute later, the vehicle approached them and slowed down. It was a brand-new green Land Rover. A man in a pair of sunglasses was behind the wheel.

His window rolled down and he barked something at them. It didn't sound Chinese.

It was Korean.

Kirina answered, "*Ne.*" That meant yes.

He gestured to the backseat. Kirina turned to Ainsley. "He said the password."

"Night swallows?"

The girl nodded.

Ainsley stooped down to get a better look at the driver. His face was impassive, his eyes hidden behind his sunglasses. He was in good health. Nothing about him indicated bad intent, but nothing reassured her either.

And how convenient it was that they should meet the one driver trawling the backroads of the North Korean border who knew the password. Then Ainsley realized something: night swallows was probably a generic password. She guessed that it was used by everyone on this side of the border who helped North Korean refugees.

In any event, Ainsley knew that they didn't have a choice. Her foot would need medical treatment quickly if she wanted to avoid infection.

"All right," she said.

The girl opened the back door, and they slipped inside the vehicle. The interior was filled with thickly cushioned tan seats. Ainsley's fingers ran over the smooth leather. The processed voice of a pop starlet sang out of high-end speakers embedded in the doors. Low bass thudded somewhere beneath her. The smell of new car enveloped her head like a wreath of sweet fog.

Ainsley felt tears coming to her eyes. The last week had been empty of the sensations of Western life. She hadn't known how much she missed them.

Ainsley looked at Kirina. The girl was sitting very still, her eyes wide open, absorbing the environment. The word luxury was unknown to her.

The driver shifted into first gear and the Range Rover began to slide quickly down the smooth asphalt. Ainsley nudged the girl. "Ask him where he's taking us."

Kirina spoke quickly in Korean. The man responded.

"He said he's taking us to a safe house," she reported.

That was all Ainsley could ask for. She lapsed into silence, looking out the window at the reddish-gray landscape, feeling the Range Rover's eight powerful cylinders humming beneath the hood.

Twenty minutes later, a two-story house appeared on the left side of the road. It was new construction, brick walls and aluminum siding, a small front lawn, flower beds. It looked totally ordinary. This home could've been found in any upper-middle class suburb anywhere in the world.

The man parked the car in the driveway. They stepped out of the car and followed him up the walk. He pulled a keycard attached to his keyfob and used it to open the front door. He gave the impression of a man who'd done this many times.

He held the door open, his face still impassive. He didn't seem to care for the two refugees, but he wasn't going out of his way to hurt them either.

As Ainsley stood in the entryway, she became aware of eyes upon her.

To her left, in what would've been the large living room, was a group of twelve bunk beds. On each mattress lay a person. All of them were looking at her.

Other North Korean refugees.

To her right was a staircase lined with young people, mostly women. They were all staring too, trying to suss out these strange newcomers. More doors extended on the second floor.

She sniffed the air. It held the fetid odor of cooked eggs and ripe garbage.

Ainsley heard the door close behind her, the electronic lock beep. The man was putting away his keyfob. He gestured to her.

She and Kirina followed him up the staircase. The women on the staircase stepped aside and studied the two newcomers.

Behind them, someone made a loud shriek. Ainsley, Kirina, and the man all turned. A middle-aged woman was pointing at a small trail of blood on the white tile floor.

It was from Ainsley's foot.

The woman looked at Ainsley accusingly, pointed at her foot, and unleashed a stream of angry Korean.

The man looked at Ainsley's foot. Then he spoke to Kirina and continued up the stairs.

"What did he say?" whispered Ainsley.

"He said he will call the medic. He will come later this afternoon."

Ainsley felt immense relief. They entered one of the upstairs bedrooms. It had three bunk beds. Two were already occupied. He pointed to the third, in the corner, then left the room.

Kirina instantly leaped up to the top bunk. Ainsley saw the girl's happiness and smiled. "How does your first day of freedom feel?"

"I want to make a big cake," the girl replied, kicking her legs in the air. "As big as a table."

"We'll do that," said Ainsley. "I'm sure there's a kitchen here."

Then she laid on the bottom bunk and felt her body sink into the mattress. The pillow was thin and the blanket even thinner, but she didn't care.

A moment later, her eyelids closed, and Ainsley was dead to the world.

CHAPTER FORTY-EIGHT

Two hours later, she awoke to the sensation of wetness on her foot. She opened her eyes.

A man was crouched at the foot of her bed. He was wearing a polo shirt and plastic medical gloves and was cleaning the bottom of her exposed foot with a wet rag. He'd also placed the limb under what seemed to be a surgical block, so that it was elevated.

"Hello," she said.

The medic was immersed in his task and didn't respond.

"Do you speak English?" she said.

Finally the medic looked up at her. Something in his eyes told her that he wasn't from China.

"You're awake," he said, in perfect English. "How was the crossing?"

"Horrible," she said.

"It's never good."

"At least I'm free."

"Almost," he said. "You're in a safe house, which isn't exactly free."

Ainsley peered at him. "Where are you from?"

"Canada," he replied. "I've been here for six weeks on a mission trip. Don't tell anybody about the mission part or I'll get booted out of the country." He studied her curiously. "Can I ask you a question?"

"Sure."

"Is your name Ainsley Walker?"

Her jaw dropped open. She was carrying no identification whatsoever. "How did you know that?"

"You don't know what's happened?"

Ainsley bolted up in bed—and hit her head on the upper mattress. She clutched her head, grimacing. "No. What's happened?"

The medic set down his instruments and reached into his pocket. He produced a phone, tapped the screen, and opened the browser. Then he typed something onto the keyboard.

"Look," he said, holding the phone up to her.

Ainsley leaned forward. He'd typed Ainsley Walker North Korea into the search engine—

—and there were over four hundred thousand results.

"The world has been talking about you," he said.

Excited, she grabbed the phone out of his hand and scrolled through the first page. Her disappearance from the Mangdonyeon Marathon in Pyongyang had become an international story. There were articles from major news outlets in every Western world—NBC, CNN, BBC, all the major newspapers, even Al Jazeera.

"The world's been looking for me?"

"You bet," he said. "The North Korean regime even told your government that you'd been taken into custody for crimes against the state."

"They're such liars!" she said. "No no no. They never got me. I was in hiding in a rural village with an elderly American man. Then they killed him, and someone else drove me to the border and we escaped over the river last night."

"The North Korean regime has been lying for twenty years," said the medic. "If it were a person, it would be classified a psychopath."

Ainsley continued scanning the news results. "Look—they even interviewed Hanna."

"Is that the Dutchwoman?"

"Yes. She's a television producer. We were roommates in Pyongyang."

The medic nodded. "The regime released her yesterday."

Ainsley flopped back onto the pillow, hand to forehead. This had blown up far bigger than she'd imagined possible.

And all for a little onyx bauble.

She reached into her pocket and pulled out the teacup and looked at it. The medic saw the object. "That's nice. Where did you buy that?"

"This little thing is the reason I went to that goddamned country in the first place." Then Ainsley paused, realizing she might've said too much. "Question. Why can't I feel my foot?"

The medic had resumed cleaning the wound. "Because I gave you a local anesthetic while you were sleeping. Do you want to hear something funny?"

"Sure."

"Me and the other missionaries—we were taking bets about whether one of us would find you."

"Really?"

He nodded. "Escaping over the Yalu River was your only decent option. Some people thought you would die."

Ainsley felt her spirits plummet. "I did not die. I survived." She paused, thinking of William. "Someone else died. He told me how to escape. He gave me the money to do it. I owe him everything." She was beginning to feel the immense weight of what had occurred.

"Either way," the medic said, "congratulations on getting the hell out. The bigger question is what now?"

She felt that question looming over her head. "I don't know. Can you help me?"

"Help you do what?"

Her hands searched the air for an answer. "I guess the first thing is, I have to get another passport. I left mine in North Korea."

"So you have to visit the U.S. consulate."

"Yeah."

"There's one in Shenyang."

"After that, I have to figure out what to do about the girl."

He pointed to the bunk above Ainsley. "Her? The pretty one?"

"Yes."

The medic glanced at the girl, started to speak, then caught his tongue. "That'll be more difficult." He turned his attention back to her foot. "So you might actually feel this. Ready?"

"Yeah."

He produced a needle from his satchel, checked it, then plunged it into her foot. It sent angry shivers through Ainsley's body. Her mouth opened, her back tensed.

"Oh my God," she said, "that stings like a—"

"It's an antibiotic. I'm taking a flyer that you've already got an infection." He dressed her foot and wrapped it in gauze. "This is the fourth foot injury I've seen in this house this month."

Ainsley understood. "So you probably know how it happened."

He nodded. "You're the only one dumb enough to jump over that fence barefoot, though."

"Hey now—"

He grinned, then shut his satchel and stood up. "Listen,

I'm gonna put the word out that you've been found. Some-body will come by to help you."

"When?"

"Very soon."

"Okay." She sat back. "What's your name?"

The medic shook his head. "It's better that you don't know."

"Because you're here on a mission trip?"

He nodded. "The Chinese don't take kindly to Christians coming to their country. It's a lot like North Korea."

"Trust me," said Ainsley, "there is no place like North Korea."

The medic laughed, then placed a package of gauze in her hand. "Change the dressing on that foot every morning for the next three days, and you should be fine. Get better, Ainsley."

"I will."

She watched the medic leave the room, then laid her head back on the pillow.

Ainsley Walker had become a celebrity.

CHAPTER FORTY-NINE

With her head buried inside the cupboards of the house kitchen, Ainsley finally found the last ingredient that she needed.

Baking powder.

Ainsley placed the small can on the countertop next to the lineup of ingredients she'd already collected—flour, eggs, sugar, and milk. This safe house had been well-stocked, thanks to well-meaning missionaries. She'd even found a mixer and a cake pan in a low drawer.

All she needed now was Kirina.

It was eleven o'clock in the morning. The girl was upstairs sleeping, just as Ainsley had been doing for most of the last twenty-four hours.

She limped upstairs to the bedroom. Kirina was still asleep, so Ainsley went over to her and gently touched her elbow.

"It's time to bake a cake," she said.

Kirina's eyes opened. "Really?"

"I have everything ready in the kitchen."

The girl stretched. "I want to take a shower first."

"Okay," said Ainsley. "You remember how I showed you to use it?"

"Yes."

"All right. I'll be waiting downstairs."

Ainsley went back to the kitchen and filled a teapot with water and set it on the stove to boil. Then she sat down to wait. She could see the people in the bunk beds watching her. They hadn't stopped doing that since she'd arrived. She reminded herself that most North Korean refugees hadn't seen a white person before.

She heard Kirina go into the bathroom upstairs. She heard the shower turn on. A few minutes later, it turned off. Then she heard a hairdryer turn on. Ainsley looked at the ingredients on the countertop. Long ago, a therapist had told her that baking was therapeutic. It was grounding. That seemed right.

Then she heard the front door open.

A pair of male voices echoed from the front of the house. She peered around the corner. It was the Range Rover driver. With him was a second man, thin, small, wearing a pinched look on his face. A pair of too-stylish red glasses perched on his nose. Ainsley instantly disliked him.

Behind them were two large men who looked like guards. They were slabs of Chinese beef.

This didn't look good.

The four men swept into the room with the twenty-four bunks. They turned over sleeping people, waking them up. The thin man roughly squeezed several women's faces, probed their mouths, inspecting them as if they were horses at auction. Ainsley could hear them talking with one another.

Then she heard a woman cry out.

Ainsley ran around the corner. They were pulling a young woman out of her bed. They bent her over and cuffed her wrists and put her down on the floor near the front door. The young woman sat crosslegged, frogtied, her long black hair hanging down the sides of her face, her body wracked with sobs.

A minute later, the muscle brought a second young woman to the door. This one resisted, so the two large guards quickly hogtied her, literally trussing her hands and her feet together as though she were going to be roasted over a fire. They put her down on the floor next to the first. Her body kicked like a fish on the bottom of a boat.

Then the four men headed upstairs.

Ainsley realized where they were headed. She limped as quickly as possible towards the stairs.

It was too late. The men were already bringing Kirina out of the bathroom. The girl's hair was wet and she looked only half-aware of what was happening. Her wrists were bound behind her body and the thin man with the red-shaded glasses had his hand on her neck.

Ainsley felt the rage building within her.

"You don't take her anywhere," she said.

As they reached the bottom of the staircase, Ainsley threw herself onto the weird man in the red glasses. One of the beefy guards pulled Ainsley off and held her against the wall one hand against her throat. She gasped for breath.

Ainsley watched helplessly as the other men led Kirina towards the front door. The Range Rover driver lifted the first girl to her feet and frogmarched her out the door. The other beefy guard picked up the second girl, the one that'd been hogtied, and threw her over his shoulder as though she were a bag of rice.

The guard released Ainsley's throat. She instantly made a last-ditch effort for Kirina. Ainsley ran across the tiled floor and threw herself onto the back of the thin man with the red-shaded glasses. Her fists flew madly, beating on the shoulders, the chest, the face.

Then she felt a larger hand fasten itself around her neck and haul her off him. It was the same beefy guard. With a flick of his arm, Ainsley flew clear across the room.

Her body slammed into the far wall. She slid to the floor, stunned.

"Kirina!" she screamed.

The owner of the Range Rover paused in the doorway, looking at Ainsley with a mixture of pity and disgust.

Then he shut the front door. Ainsley heard the engine start up in the driveway and the vehicle pull away.

Kirina was gone. Less than three minutes was all it took.

She buried her face in her hands. All that effort she'd gone through to get the girl safely out of North Korea to freedom —it was all for nothing.

Ainsley hung her head between her knees. The front door beeped and opened. She heard the owner of the Range Rover explaining something.

Then she heard a male voice respond. It sounded vaguely familiar, as though it belonged to someone she had known in a dream.

She lifted her head.

Standing before her was Pastor Jeong.

CHAPTER FIFTY

Ainsley looked at him, stunned. Words came to her lips, then disappeared. He was dressed in an anonymous black coat and black pants, as though he were hiding in plain sight.

"Ainsley Walker," he said, "it gives me great relief to see that you escaped."

"You screwed me," she replied.

He cleared his throat. "I'm sorry that you had a difficult experience, Miss Walker."

The minister offered his hand. Ignoring it, she pulled herself up to a standing position. "You told me that Kenneth Park would pass me the onyx teacup at the marathon. You told me that."

"That was the plan—"

"But he didn't! Do you know what he did? He handed me a goddamned note that told me that the goddamned regime was coming for me!"

The minister was the very picture of humility. "I deeply apologize. There must have been a miscommunication."

"I'd say so."

"We are prepared to offer you a bonus for your troubles."

"Double it, and I accept." She studied his inscrutable face. "Why are you here? In China?"

"I'm a missionary," he said. "I often travel here to help my people after they escape."

"And you knew that I would escape over the river?"

He nodded. "We saw the media reports about your disappearance, and I hoped that you would learn to escape in the way that everybody does."

"Which I did, thanks to William Yaris."

She saw his face change, only for a moment. It was a microexpression of discomfort. "Who is Mister Yaris?"

"He's the elderly American who helped us to escape."

"Us?"

"The girl, Kirina. That's his daughter. Those goons dragged her out a minute ago. You must've seen her in the driveway."

He nodded. "I did. A pretty girl." He changed the subject, grew more delicate. "So did you ever find the onyx teacup?"

That was her ace in the pocket. Ainsley wasn't going to give him the satisfaction of finding that out, not yet. She was going to make him wait.

"First, tell me where they are taking the girl."

His face grew sad. "She will be sold as a bride."

Ainsley looked at him. Her eyes flicked back and forth across his face to assess the truth. "But she's only twelve years old."

"The traders don't care. To them, the younger, the better. About seventy-five percent of the girls who escape North Korea and cross the border get sold as wives." He gestured around to the house. "Many of these women will be selected eventually. They have no choice because they don't have the *hukou*."

"What's that?"

"Chinese identification."

Ainsley felt her gut tighten inside. "So who buys the girls?"

"Chinese farmers, mostly."

She tried to imagine the girl being carried out to remote village in some Chinese province, to live the rest of her life in a primitive hut, farming a garden. She reassured herself that at least it would be familiar territory to Kirina.

"Kirina is too pretty to live on a farm."

"The beautiful ones go to rich men in cities all over the world. They pay much more." The minister lifted his palms in a gesture of acceptance. "There was nothing you could do."

"That girl saved my life—"

He lowered his voice. "Ainsley, listen to me."

"What?"

"They wanted to take you too."

He let that sink in. It did. She felt her stomach drop. Being sold into slavery was inconceivable. She was a free woman, always had been, always would be.

"But I'm twenty-nine. And I'm American. Why would somebody want to buy me?"

"Japanese brothels love to buy American women, especially blondes. It's happened before."

Her eyes narrowed. "So why didn't they take me?"

A knowing look came over the pastor's face. "Because I bargained for you. That's why I had to give up the girl."

Ainsley felt a wave of gratitude sweep over her body. If he could be believed, Pastor Jeong had gone out of his way to save her life.

"I guess that makes things even."

He held up a hand. "It was the least I could do."

That seemed fair. Then she suddenly grew suspicious. "Of course, it's convenient that I also found the onyx teacup."

He didn't say anything, but his eyes flashed with life. "Yes, I saved you for that reason too. But don't be so cynical." His tongue wetted his lips and he chose his next words carefully. "So you have the teacup with you?"

His eyes looked at her probingly. In the kitchen, Ainsley heard the teapot begin to whistle.

"Maybe," she said. "Let's have some tea and discuss it."

CHAPTER FIFTY-ONE

Ainsley limped into the kitchen, the minister behind her. She turned on the switch, and the light fixture hanging over the long kitchen table exploded into a bright light.

"Sit there," she said, pointing at a seat.

Pastor Jeong obeyed. He folded his hands primly upon the table and waited.

Ainsley went over to the pantry and found a porcelain teacup and brought it over and placed it in front of him. Then she brought over the teapot and sat down.

"Aren't you having any tea?" he said.

Without a word, Ainsley unzipped the pocket of her jacket, produced the onyx teacup, and placed it on the table.

The overhead light caught the gemstone nicely. Pastor Jeong's face lit up.

They both studied the gemstone. This was the first time she'd ever really looked at the teacup in the light. It had a thick base and a shallow bowl and was a deep purplish black. The process of selective absorption filtered out everything except the darkest end of the chromatic spectrum.

"It's beautiful," he said.

Ainsley solemnly poured the tea into his porcelain cup. Then she poured her own tea into the onyx teacup.

Pastor Jeong's eyes went wide as he watched the liquid fill the onyx. He lifted a nervous hand to his face, then put it down, then shifted uncomfortably in his seat.

She lifted it. "To a successful mission."

He lifted his teacup. "To a successful mission."

They both sipped the tea. His eyes remained fixated on the black treasure.

"Now," she said, "why don't you tell me the real reason you want this onyx."

Pastor Jeong was caught flatfooted. His larynx worked itself oddly in his throat. His lips contracted, then relaxed. Beads of sweat formed along his hairline.

Ainsley was enjoying this.

He stuck to the party line. "You already know, Miss Walker. We have to save our church. We have an arrangement with Ji-hoon Kwon to buy it because—"

"That's a lie."

Ainsley waited for his reaction. His eyes were squirming left and right. They seemed to be physically withdrawing into his skull.

"I don't know what you mean," he said.

Ainsley leaned forward and fixed him with a stare. "What I mean is that your grandfather never hid this onyx teacup because he never possessed it. And Ji-hoon Kwon isn't going to buy it from you because you don't even know him." She narrowed her eyes. "In fact, I wonder if your little church is even real."

He made a small pfft sound. "Your suspicions are preposterous."

"They are preposterous," said Ainsley, "and even worse, I think they're true."

A strange smirk appeared on the pastor's face. "You have a fanciful imagination, Miss Walker—"

"Tell me I'm wrong."

The minister fell silent. His eyes glanced at her own, then flitted away. She sensed that he was about to break.

"What if you're right?" he said. "What do we do then?"

A knowing look had appeared on his face. Ainsley sat back in her chair, stunned. For the last week, she'd suspected exactly as much. Kenneth Park's strange note. William Yaris' offhand comments. The plan to smuggle the teacup out of the country by covering it in clay. In short, a woman knows when she's being lied to, and Ainsley's radar had been pinging loudly.

"Tell me what I was really doing in North Korea."

The man's eyes glanced at the onyx teacup. He cleared his throat. "If you empty your cup, I will be happy to show you."

By this time, a small crowd of fellow refugees had gathered around the table. Ainsley didn't discourage them. It would be good to have witnesses, just in case.

Ainsley lifted the teacup to her lips and drained the last of the liquid. She hesitated before handing it over.

"You rented a car, right?" she said.

"Yes."

"Give me your car key."

"Why?"

"Collateral."

The minister reluctantly produced a rental car key from his pocket and placed it on the table. Ainsley swept it into her lap.

Then she handed him the onyx teacup.

The pastor's eyes grew very focused as he handled the object, holding it up to the light, studying its contours, twisting it around.

She grew impatient. "What are you going to show me?"

"This."

He turned the cup upside down. His fingers felt intently around the base of the gemstone. They pressed two spots, then squeezed two different spots. Finally he pressed his thumb down upon the base of the teacup.

It made a small click.

Pastor Jeong slowly began to unscrew the false bottom of the teacup. He removed the onyx plate and laid it gently upon the table.

Ainsley gulped nervously. A small *ooh* sounded from the onlookers.

"This," he said, "is what you were doing in North Korea."

He reached into the bottom of the teacup and gently removed something. He held it up between two fingertips for Ainsley to see.

It was a tiny printed circuit board.

Ainsley felt her throat go dry. "What is that?"

"A flash drive," he said. "It's the same kind you can buy at any store. We just took off the plastic case."

Ainsley felt the room beginning to spin. She clutched the table to slow it down. "What's on the flash drive?"

"I don't know."

Her heart was pounding like a wild animal trying to escape her chest. She fought to keep her voice even. "No, I think you do."

His eyes, normally so placid, were dancing now. "I really don't, not exactly. Kenneth Park could've told you."

"That wasn't his real name, was it?"

He shook his head no.

"And you're not really a pastor, are you?"

The man shook his head again.

"Can I guess who you really are?"

"No."

"Why not?"

"Because you'll probably be right."

She heard herself say it anyways. "I think you work for the CIA."

He said nothing.

"The Central Intelligence Agency," she said, "just to be clear."

The man remained totally silent. His eyes were fixed upon her own, daring her to continue.

"You used me to smuggle your secrets out of North Korea. You played me like a cheap piano. Everything you told me was a lie."

On the other side of the table, the man shrugged. "I couldn't tell you what was really happening. It was for everybody's good."

"Why not?"

"In case you were detained by the regime."

Ainsley sat back. "Tell me, what would have happened if they'd arrested me? What would you have done?"

The man sighed. "First, back-channel negotiations. If that didn't work, we would've sent a former politician or important official to beg. Sometimes that's the only way the bastards will release anybody." The man paused. "By the way, your friend Hanna was released this morning."

"I heard."

"But only after the former prime minister of the Netherlands intervened on her behalf."

Ainsley felt a second wave of relief wash over her. Hanna had been a good egg. She hadn't deserved to die in a foreign prison.

She watched him place the flash drive in a small case, close it securely, and stow it away in his shirt pocket. Then he handed Ainsley the onyx teacup.

"You can keep it," he said.

She accepted the object. It would remind her not to be so

gullible in the future. Adventure wasn't everything in life. Staying home, staying warm, and staying alive were important too.

"Is this really onyx?" she said.

"I don't know. You can ask the lab that gave it to me."

"Why a teacup?"

"I don't know the details, but you can figure it out."

Ainsley thought about it. It would be an ideal way to smuggle something out of a high-security area, especially in a country where tea drinking was such an accepted part of life.

The man formerly known as Pastor Jeong got to his feet. "Now, if you'll follow me outside, we'll get you to a consulate and find you a new passport."

"I'm not going anywhere with you," she said.

The man smiled at her sadly. "Ainsley, the second I leave, they call the traders back and you get sold to an Asian brothel."

Ainsley felt defeated. This was her best option.

She pulled herself to her feet and padded over to the front door where her pink-and-white trainers stood out in the pile of sad North Korean footwear. She felt the other refugees' jealous eyes burning into her neck. There was nothing she could do for them.

She put on her running top, picked up her bag, and followed Pastor Jeong out of the house.

EPILOGUE

They approached the rental car, a Honda. It was parked on the edge of the street. Ainsley held the key in her pocket.

"Could I have my key, please?" he said.

"Not until you tell me more about William Yaris."

The pair stood there in the middle of the two-lane road. It was a cold morning, and Ainsley fought off the shivers.

The man sighed. "The truth?"

"Yes."

"He's the deepest agent we currently have in North Korea. He repaid our country many times over for his youthful sin."

That didn't surprise her. Nothing did about this case. "He's not your deepest agent anymore," she said.

"Why?"

"They killed him."

The man stopped. "Did you see it?"

She nodded. "It was a public execution in his village." She felt her throat catch. "With a flamethrower."

He lowered his head, seeming genuinely sad. "That is a blow. He was irreplaceable."

Ainsley thought about him. William Yaris had known exactly the value of the thumb drive inside that onyx teacup, which is why he'd given it to his daughter—the only person he could trust—to hide it in the mountains. Then he waited for a way to get it out of the country. That was conveniently accomplished by Ainsley, under the pretext of smuggling his daughter out, which is what he'd wanted anyways. The old man had been able to kill two birds with one stone. She consoled herself knowing that he'd died a happy man.

"So who is Kenneth Park?" she said.

"He was our connection to Yaris after Yaris fell out of favor with the regime and lost some of his freedoms." He cleared his throat. "Ainsley, you surprised all of us at the agency. Honestly, nobody thought that you could accomplish this. We thought you'd either die, be captured, or come back with empty pockets."

"So I was a last-ditch effort."

"Basically. And the secrets on this thumb drive will help the world defeat the entire regime. It's all because of you."

That was the story of Ainsley's life. She was the girl who followed the distant beat of her own distant drummer, the one that nobody thought she would ever amount to anything special—until they witnessed her boldness, savviness, and persistence.

He tilted his head and studied her. "You've lost weight."

She crossed her arms over her chest. "I know."

"Give me the car key."

She hesitated.

"I guess you don't like food anymore."

She ticked off on her fingers all of her needs. "I need so many things. I need a new passport, new clothes, a new plane ticket—"

"We'll do all of it," he said, "trust me. I flew all the way to China for you."

"You flew all the way to China for the onyx teacup."

"And for you."

Ainsley finally threw his car key back at him. He caught it in midair.

Then he paused. His mobile phone had beeped. As he fished out the device and read the screen, Ainsley stood there in the street, feeling cold and confused. She was still processing the extent to which she'd been duped in the name of national security. It was a lot to take in, and it would take time to fully sink in.

"Ainsley," he said, looking at his phone, "would you be interested in another assignment?"

Her ears perked up. "Maybe."

He looked at his phone. "There seems to be a problem nearby."

"Where?"

"Mongolia."

Her brow creased. "What the hell is in Mongolia?"

"What the hell is in North Korea?" he countered.

She smiled. "Yeah, good point."

"I'll tell you about it on the way."

He unlocked the vehicle. Ainsley opened the passenger door and slipped inside.

PLOTWORKS PUBLISHING

If you enjoyed this story, please leave a review at the place where you purchased it.

Then visit Plotworks Publishing to follow Ainsley Walker on her next exciting gemstone travel mystery, *The Mongolian Moonstone*!

Now turn the page for a sneak peek—

THE MONGOLIAN MOONSTONE

J.A. JERNAY

THE MONGOLIAN MOONSTONE

The sun fell towards the horizon, washing the landscape in a bath of pink and orange hues.

The silver Range Rover idled on the dirt track near Tungdik's ger. The small round tent was colored a rich purple. It was nestled into the lip of a hillside.

Erdene looked over at Harriet. "Are you sure this is it?"

"I think so."

"I don't want to spend a night with the wrong family."

Harriet pored over the map in her lap. "I've doublechecked. This is the valley."

"Was it purple?"

"I don't know."

"Shouldn't we make a camp?" said Ainsley. "It's almost dark."

Erdene looked at her. "We're staying with Tungdik."

"But we don't know him. Only Harriet knows him."

The naturalist turned around in the seat. "Ainsley, it's customary in the steppe for nomads to accept all travelers."

"It's the Mongolian way," added Erdene.

"So we just knock on their door and ask for a bed?"

"Yes," said Erdene.

"Oh," said Ainsley. Approaching a stranger's house at sunset, knowing that that person would be required to accept you for the night, was going to require some getting used to.

Harriet folded the map. "I think this is it, Erdene. Everything seems to correspond."

Erdene shifted into first and turned the wheel. The vehicle rolled off the dirt track and onto the grass.

Ahead, the purple ger grew larger. A couple additional ones grew visible behind it.

When they were a couple hundred meters away, Erdene stopped the car. "Let's get out here and approach on foot."

They stepped out of the car. It was a glorious sunset and nearly as glorious a meadow. Around them stretched a carpet of wild grasses that gently sloped down to the edge of a blue lake about a kilometer away. On the other side of the flat blue water stood a small mountain range.

A sheep's bleat sounded distantly across the grass. Ainsley turned her eyes back to the land. It was sprinkled with livestock—cows, sheep, and goats.

Harriet came and stood next Ainsley. "What do you think?"

"It's gorgeous."

The naturalist sucked on a tooth. "I've seen better."

"You must be joking."

"No, I'm quite serious. There's even better land about a hundred kilometers west of here."

The three women crossed the grass. "Do you remember our roles here, Ainsley?" said Erdene.

Ainsley did remember. "This is a cultural exchange. I'm the tourist, you're the guide."

"What should I be?" said Harriet.

Erdene stroked her chin. "Didn't they already meet you?"

"Yes."

"Then just be yourself."

Harriet nodded briskly. "British naturalist, check."

———

At the ger, a nomadic herdsman was sitting on a small stool outside the front door. He was calmly stropping a knife on a piece of worn leather.

As they approached him, Erdene stopped and cupped her hands around her mouth. "*Nokhoi khor!*"

"That means *hold your dog*," explained Harriet. "It's the first thing you always say when you arrive."

The man stood and shouted something back.

"He said he doesn't have any," said Harriet.

"Is that Tungdik?" said Erdene.

The Englishwoman looked unsure. "I really need to get closer."

"If it's not, we have to back out right now, before he extends any hospitality."

Harriet looked the man. "Lord, I don't really remember. But he was missing a couple of his front teeth."

They moved towards the Mongol herder, and he moved towards them. The man was large. He wore a Western-style red parka with extra-long sleeves, a pair of blue jeans, and a pair of simple work boots. On his face, a smile struggled to lift his sagging cheeks. Ainsley glimpsed a gap in his front teeth.

"That's him," said Ainsley.

"Yes," said Harriet. "He has a wife and a thirteen-year-old son who is a bit large for his age."

Tungdik shook each of their hands. His own was callused and ridged and felt like a plaster sculpture. He and Erdene chattered in rapidfire Mongolian, as if they were old friends.

Then he pointed towards the ger and gestured for them to follow him.

"Ready or not, we are now guests," said Harriet. "Is this your first time in a ger?"

"It is," said Ainsley.

She grinned. "Prepare yourself."

PLOTWORKS PUBLISHING

Visit Plotworks Publishing to follow Ainsley Walker on her next exciting gemstone travel mystery!

Then explore a new series by J.A. Jernay—the Cosmo Bennett Mapping Thrillers!

Turn the page for another sneak peek—

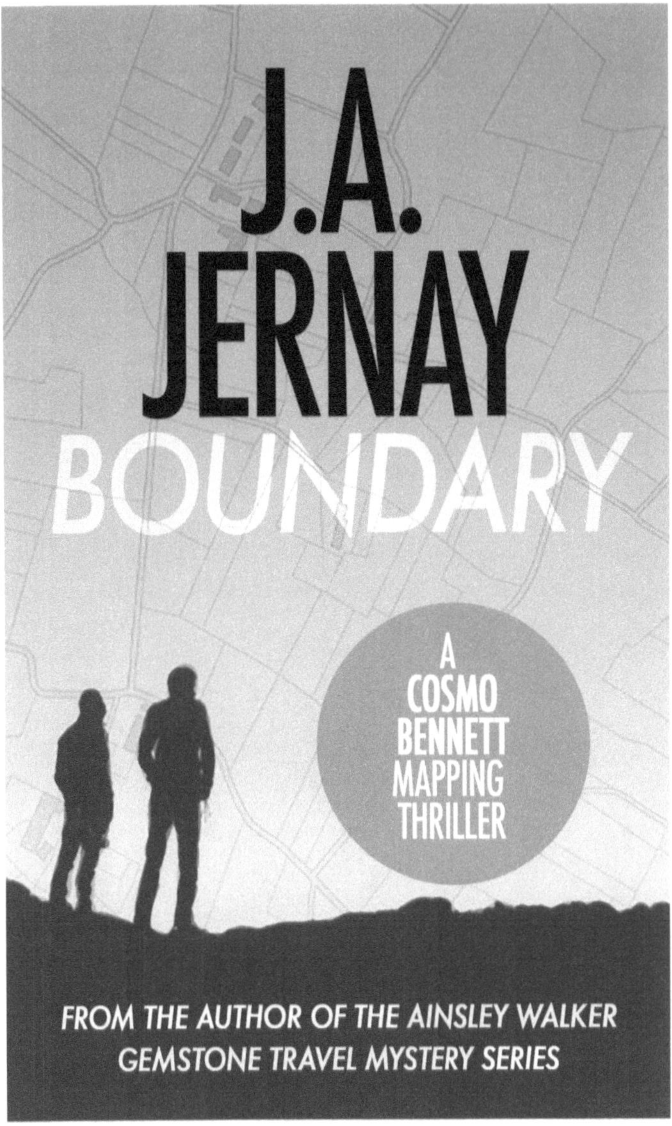
J.A.
JERNAY
BOUNDARY
A
COSMO
BENNETT
MAPPING
THRILLER
FROM THE AUTHOR OF THE AINSLEY WALKER
GEMSTONE TRAVEL MYSTERY SERIES

BOUNDARY

Cosmo and his assistant Noah shuffled down the dirt shoulder of the boulevard in the midday heat, sweating and miserable.

Each was lost in his own thoughts. Cosmo dreamed of hitting a heavy punching bag at his gymnasium. Noah dreamed of passing level nineteen of Operation Earlobe, an obscure RPG he'd abandoned last semester.

The morning's meeting had been a complete bust.

"I don't think we should continue," said Cosmo finally.

Noah didn't respond, but Cosmo took no notice. He continued: "I don't think anybody here takes our task seriously. I don't think this propaganda map was as influential as they say. I don't think this map has driven the civil unrest. I think social media and centuries of tribal warfare are more to blame for the unrest than anything else."

He looked over at Noah, waiting for a response. "What about you?"

The graduate assistant came back from his reverie. "Huh?"

"Did you hear anything I said?"

"No."

"I was just saying this is pointless and we should go home."

"I don't have a problem with that."

They arrived at Vida e Caffe. It was a chain café, with hundreds of similar franchises scattered across the southern half of the African continent. The branding was modern and inviting. A hundred people sat beneath umbrellas at small tables on the large outdoor patio.

An arm was waving at them. It was Christopher, their fixer, a cup of tea on a ceramic saucer in front of him. Two other cups awaited them.

"Hello sirs," he said. "I ordered us all a rooibos. It's a vanilla tea that is extraordinary."

Cosmo and Noah pulled out the chairs and sat down. The driver quickly sussed out that something was wrong.

"It was a bad meeting?" he said quietly.

"Yes," said Cosmo, "there was no progress made."

"I'm very sorry."

Cosmo sighed. "I think we have to leave."

The fixer looked confused. "But you just sat down—"

"The country," he clarified. "We have to leave Fabajouti. We can't seem to do any good here."

Christopher looked crestfallen. "I do understand your frustration."

Noah said, "If it's okay with you, we'd probably like to just get in the car and go back to the hotel."

The fixer rediscovered his manners. "Of course, as you wish—"

"But we'd love to try the tea first—" added Cosmo.

"You two enjoy the rooibos," said Christopher, "while I fetch the car. The parking lot is very jammed and it will take quite a while to remove. I've already paid the bill."

Before they could object, the driver had shot to his feet.

He clapped Cosmo on the shoulder and left the patio. They watched him cross the boulevard to an off-street parking area that was crammed tightly with vehicles. On his approach, the attendant began shifting other vehicles.

Noah sipped the tea. "This does taste really good. I don't drink enough tea."

"I like tea," said Cosmo. He sipped from the cup. "This one is good."

"What's your favorite?" asked Noah.

"Maybe pu'er."

"That one's bitter, right?"

"Yeah. It's fermented."

"What about Earl Grey?"

"A cliché."

"I think I'm more of a fruity tea guy," said Noah.

Cosmo nodded. "Yeah, they have their charms."

"You ever try chamomile?"

"It's good for sleeping," said Cosmo, "but otherwise it's—"

His comment was cut short by a massive fireball that erupted from the parking lot across the street.

———

In a split second, Cosmo and Noah instinctively rolled off their chairs and onto the ground beneath their table. Their eyes met. Each was filled with terror.

Then the shock of the overpressure hit. Cosmo felt the force of the blast wave hit the left side of his body. The highly compressed air rattled the left side of his skull. It even sent his lips and cheeks flapping to the right.

The initial sound of the explosion was deafening, but that was soon replaced by a symphony of falling destruction. A thousand pieces of metal, plastic, glass, and upholstery rained down upon the boulevard, the grass, the other cars.

A shower of tiny shrapnel hit on the patio of the cafe. One hit Noah in the hand and sizzled his flesh. He shook it off.

They waited another few seconds for the shrapnel rain to end. Then Cosmo and Noah lifted their heads.

The patio of the café was transformed into pandemonium. The patrons started to pull themselves up from the ground and flee out to the street and in the opposite direction. The street itself was coming alive with panicked people running in every direction.

"What the actual—" said Noah.

"Christopher!" interrupted Cosmo. "What about Christopher?"

He scrambled up to his feet. Without waiting for Noah, he sprinted out of the café and across the boulevard, weaving through the stopped cars. The air was acrid with chemicals and the heat had somehow intensified even further.

The parking lot was a field of wreckage. The bomb had exploded in the middle of the space, shredding every vehicle and person within twenty meters. Pieces of concrete and metal and glass had been blown across the scene.

"Christopher!" he shouted again. "Christopher! Don't do this!"

He saw a shoe with a foot still in it. He saw a red string of guts entangled in a hubcap. A wave of nausea gripped his stomach. He covered his nose with his t-shirt and backed away.

He tripped backwards over a piece of metal, stumbled, and fell to the ground.

That's when he saw it.

A long strip of shredded fabric. A yellow-and-green printed tropical shirt.

It was bloody and torn.

Cosmo turned his head and retched onto the asphalt. All the tea he'd just drank came out.

He somehow pulled himself to his feet and staggered back to the café. Noah was waiting at the far corner, on the sidewalk, pacing frantically.

"So?"

"I found him," said Cosmo. He forced the next words out. "A little bit."

Noah's face went white. "Oh my God."

Cosmo didn't say anything. He just gripped Noah by the upper arm. "Walk with me. And don't look back."

———

The pair moved briskly down the boulevard, away from the scene. People were running past them, mouths open, eyes full of fear, but Cosmo maintained a steady pace. His face betrayed an intense desire to appear as normal as possible.

"So we're just going to leave the scene?" said Noah.

"Yep."

"Why?"

"Don't make me answer that, Noah."

"I think we should talk to the police, cooperate, tell them everything—"

"In a different country," Cosmo replied, "in a different scenario, you'd be right. But not here, not now."

Noah looked back over his shoulder at the scene.

"Look straight ahead," Cosmo said through his teeth, "and listen to me. Our Mercedes is gone. Christopher is ... gone."

"Shit—"

"And I'm going to suggest something else that could blow your mind."

"What?"

"It's possible that we were the intended target."

"That's insane."

"Is it?"

"How do you know?"

"I don't. But it's a possibility. Here's another one. It's possible that we are going to be used as scapegoats. We were the last people seen eating with Christopher. Do you want to be put in a Fabajouti jail on suspicion of a crime?"

They walked for another half minute in silence. Behind them, the chaos grew distant.

"Where are we going?" Noah said finally.

"Back to the hotel."

"And then?"

"We're leaving, like we planned."

"We're not going home, are we?" said Noah.

Cosmo's mouth grew hard and his jaw jutted out. He stared straight forward at an invisible point on the horizon. "No, we're not."

PLOTWORKS PUBLISHING

Visit Plotworks Publishing today to find all these titles—and more!